Vibrant, exotic settings!
Powerful family dynasties!
Brooding Outback bachelors!
Spirited women who fight for
the men they love!

MARGARET WAY

Loved around the world for her dramatic
and daring, tempestuous and timeless novels.

If you haven't joined the millions of women
who love Margaret Way's stories,
try one now!

Praise for the author:

"Margaret Way has over 80 books in print; all with
a few things in common: glorious scenery, strong
characters, and a powerful style of writing that keeps
the reader turning the pages to see how it will end."
—Diane Grayson, *www.theromancereader.com*

"With climactic scenes, dramatic imagery
and bold characters, Margaret Way
makes the Outback come alive."
—*RT Book Reviews*

MARGARET WAY

Outback Bachelor

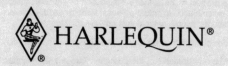

HARLEQUIN®

TORONTO • NEW YORK • LONDON
AMSTERDAM • PARIS • SYDNEY • HAMBURG
STOCKHOLM • ATHENS • TOKYO • MILAN • MADRID
PRAGUE • WARSAW • BUDAPEST • AUCKLAND

Recycling programs for this product may not exist in your area.

ISBN-13: 978-0-373-17643-4

OUTBACK BACHELOR

First North American Publication 2010.

www.eHarlequin.com

Printed in U.S.A.

Margaret Way, a definite Leo, was born and raised in the subtropical River City of Brisbane, capital of the Sunshine State of Queensland. A Conservatorium-trained pianist, teacher, accompanist and vocal coach, she found her musical career came to an unexpected end when she took up writing—initially as a fun thing to do. She currently lives in a harborside apartment at beautiful Raby Bay, a thirty-minute drive from the state capital, where she loves dining alfresco on her plant-filled balcony, overlooking a translucent green marina filled with all manner of pleasure craft—from motor cruisers costing millions of dollars, and big, graceful yachts with carved masts standing tall against the cloudless blue sky, to little bay runabouts. No one and nothing is in a mad rush, and she finds the laid-back village atmosphere very conducive to her writing. With well over a hundred books to her credit, she still believes her best is yet to come.

PROLOGUE

THE night before she was to make her sad journey back to Djinjara, after a self-imposed absence, Skye's dreams were filled with vivid childhood memories of life on the great station. Those had been the halcyon days when Djinjara had been the centre of her universe, the days before she had become overpowered by the McGoverns, cattle barons prominent among the nation's great landed families. Broderick McGovern had been master of Djinjara when she had been growing up; a man with tremendous obligations and responsibilities, greatly respected by all. Keefe, his elder son, had been the heir. Scott, next in line, the difficult one, burdened with sibling rivalry issues, always making it his business to stir up discord. Rachelle, the youngest, was rather good at stirring up trouble herself, but happily for the McGovern dynasty Keefe was everything he was supposed to be. And much more.

By the time she was five she had fallen totally under his spell. She couldn't imagine life without Keefe in it! A deprived child, struggling with the loss of a mother and a mother's love and guidance, she found Keefe to be a source of continual comfort, delight and admiration. He commanded her world. It was a role her hard-working, grieving father didn't seem able to fill. At least not for a long time. Skye's father, Jack McCory, was a man who had never come to terms with losing his beautiful young wife Cathy in childbirth. Thereafter, he lamented it would never have happened only Cathy had insisted on having her child on the station instead of at Base Hospital.

By such decisions was our fate determined.

In her early years Skye couldn't understand her father's deep melancholy, neither as a child could she be expected to, though she always tried to ease it by being a good girl and putting her mind to her lessons at the station school. Her teacher, Mrs. Lacey, always embarrassed her, instructing the other children, offspring of station employees, *"Let Skye be an example to you!"*

With Mrs. Lacey, an excellent teacher, she could do no wrong. *"Why shouldn't she praise you?"* Keefe commented lazily when she complained. *"You're one bright little kid. And you're really, really pretty!"* This with a playful tug on her blonde curls. Keefe was six years her senior. From age ten he had been sent as a boarder to his illustrious private school in Sydney. The times he was home on vacation were, therefore, doubly precious to her.

Times changed. People changed with them. It wasn't unusual for the bonds of childhood not to survive into adulthood. By the time Keefe became a man he was no longer the Keefe who had laughed at her, listened to her, tolerated her showing-off, taken her up on his shoulders while she squealed her pleasure at the top of her lungs. The *adult* Keefe not only filled her with awe, he came close to daunting her. Even when he was looking straight at her she imagined he was looking *through* her. Something absolutely fundamental between them had changed. What made it all that much harder to bear was it seemed to happen overnight.

Their respective roles became blindingly clear.

She could never, not *ever,* enter Keefe McGovern's adult world.

Despite her strenuous efforts to distance herself, and make her own way in life, Keefe continued to live on in her mind and her dreams. He was her shooting star, with all a star's grandeur. Not with the best will in the world could she change that. Obsessions, unlike many friendships, remained constant.

It had been devastation of a kind after she had made the break to go to university. It had become very important for her to separate herself from the McGoverns. Separate from Keefe, her hero. Even the thought made her weep, but her tears fell silently down the walls of her heart.

Keefe! Oh, Keefe!

Had *it* really happened those few years ago, or had she imagined it all? *Remember.* Oh, yes it had happened.

No young men she had met thereafter—and she had met many who were attracted to her—could measure up to Keefe. Now twenty-four she was making a success of her life even if she continued to feel deeply obligated to the McGoverns. Their interest in her had secured her bright future. McGovern money had paid for her expensive education. Her father explained years later that Lady McGovern, grandmother to Keefe, Scott and Rachelle, had insisted that fact be keep quiet.

"*Skye is not to know. But she's such a clever child she must be given the best possible chance in life.*"

Although Lady McGovern had always been a majestic figure, as aloof as royalty, in all truth she had been oddly protective of a lowly employee's young daughter. That alone had caused the ever-deepening rift between Rachelle and herself. Rachelle had a jealous nature. She loved both her brothers, but it was Keefe she adored. It was Keefe's attention Rachelle always fought for. If it were true that some mothers couldn't give up their sons to girlfriends and wives, it was equally true that some sisters were unwilling to take a back seat in their brother's affections. Rachelle hung in there, determined Skye would never be allowed to stake a claim on the family. Skye was always *"the pushy little daughter of—can you believe— a station hand? Always trying to ingratiate yourself with our family."* Reading between the lines, that meant Rachelle's adored brother, Keefe. These were just a couple of the insults Rachelle tossed off like barbed arrows.

Over time, the insults worsened.

"You're to be pitied. You may be chocolate-box pretty, but you're so disadvantaged by your background. You'll never be accepted into our world. So don't even try!" The tone Rachelle employed was so caustic she might have been trying to skin the younger girl alive. Skye learned early in life all about jealousy. It was to her credit such jealousy hadn't crushed her. Rather, the reverse. She learned to stand up for herself. McGovern wealth, status and their pastoral empire gave them uncommon power. They certainly had power over her. Even in her dreams Keefe and Djinjara didn't let go.

As she lay sleeping on that heated and stormy November evening, with the air-conditioner running full blast, she became trapped in that idyllic past as images began to flood her mind. So vivid were they, they brought into play all five of her senses. She could actually *smell* things, *feel* things, *hear* things, *taste* things. She could *see* all the rich colours, observe the legions of tiny emerald and gold budgies that flew overhead in their perfect squadron formations. It was stunning how clearly she was able to open a window on the past, a traveller in time…

She was five and back on Djinjara. Her father Jack was then a Djinjara stockman, later a leading hand, rising to overseer by the time she was ten. It was around about puberty that life abruptly became *different.* Suddenly out of nowhere she felt the weight of strange longings; an urgency and a hunger for sight and sound of Keefe, a pressing need for his company.

She only saw him when they came together in the school vacations. It was way too long in between. What she was feeling, had she known it, was desire, but she was too young to recognise it. That was as well, for it was ill advised. Whatever Skye desired, it was never going to happen. Her intuitive response was to modify her warm, open manner to avoid embarrassing herself and, God forbid, Keefe.

In the academic year following her twelfth birthday she was stunned to learn she was to be sent away to Rachelle's prestigious girl's school. She had never thought such a thing could happen. The fees alone were way, way beyond her father's modest means; the choice of such a college not even considered by a parent in Jack McCory's position in life. This was a school for the social elite.

It took Skye years to find out the McGoverns had paid the fees. But back then, to make her father proud, she had worked very hard, graduating five years later with a top score. That score had enabled her to go to the university of her choice and study law. Her driving interest had become women's affairs. She wanted to be in a position to help women facing serious legal problems, especially women facing such problems alone.

In her dream that hot, humid night, she was a child again, standing transfixed, holding fast to Keefe's hand. They were looking out on an enchanted world of wildflowers. Never in her short life had she seen such an extraordinary spectacle! It was so beautiful it made her heart ache.

"The miracle after years of drought!" Keefe's voice lifted on a note of pride and elation. *"The desert wildflowers have arrived, little buddy!"* He often called her "little buddy" in those days. It was like real affection flowed between her and this Outback prince. That year, when she turned five, the flowers were out in their millions. They came in the wake of a major cyclone in the tropical Far North. The run-off flood-

waters poured in great torrents down the interior's Three Rivers System. They reached right into the Red Heart, spilling out of the infinite maze of intricate, interlocking waterways of the Channel Country, bringing great rejoicing even though station after station was left stranded in an inland sea.

In her dream, the flowers blazed their way across the great golden spinifex plains, climbed the fiery red pyramids of the sand dunes, spread right to the feet of the distant hills that always appeared to her child's eye like ruined castles full of mystery and past splendours. The flowers were dazzling white, bright yellow, all the pinks and oranges, mauve into violet, vibrant reds, their colours dancing in the breeze. They were the loveliest creations she had ever seen, their beauty hazy under the golden desert sun.

"Thought you might like to see them." Keefe smiled down at her, pleased with her evident excitement, an excitement he shared. Marvellously handsome and clever, he was home for the long Christmas-New Year vacation.

"Oh, Keefe, it's *magic!*" She clapped her hands, transported out of herself with joy. Even at that age she felt deeply. *"Thank you, thank you, for bringing me."*

"No need to thank me. I knew how much you'd love it. You're our little Outback princess."

In retrospect it was a very strange thing for him to say, though as a five-year-old she accepted it as a joke. In return she gave him her purest little girl smile, thrilled and excited he had thought of her. Really, she was just another little kid on the station, yet he had actually come in search of her, taking her up before him on his beautiful, fleet-footed thoroughbred mare, Noor, one of the finest in Djinjara's stables. Keefe could ride her. Keefe could ride anything. He was tall for his age, with the promise of attaining over six feet in manhood.

In her dream he was holding firmly to her hand lest she run

excitedly into the shimmering sea of paper daisies that could easily shelter a dragon lizard that might not take kindly to being disturbed. Keefe was there to protect her as well as show her the wild flowers. He was no ordinary boy. He didn't look it. He didn't sound it. Even then he had been one of those people with enormous charisma. And why not? He was Keefe McGovern, heir to Djinjara.

Her father was often required to go away on long musters, leaving Skye for days, sometimes weeks. She was almost an orphan, except everyone on the station looked out for her. She even had a nanny called Lena, a gentle, mission-educated aboriginal lady appointed by Lady McGovern, stern matriarch of the family. When her father was away on those long musters Lady McGovern allowed her and Lena to stay at the Big House. That was the name everyone on the station called Djinjara homestead. It was a *palace*, so grand and immense! She and her dad lived in a little bungalow that would have just about fitted into Djinjara's entrance hall. Her dad had impressed on her that it was a "great honour" to be allowed to stay at the Big House. So she had to be a good girl.

It was easy. No one upset or frightened her. Well…Rachelle did, but she was finding her way around that. There was something nasty about Rachelle, two years her senior. But even though she was little, Rachelle didn't intimidate her. It was her duty to be a good, brave girl and not worry her father, who worked so hard.

In her dreamscape she was weaving her small fingers in and out of Keefe's strong brown hand. *"I really love you, Keefe."*

He smiled, his light eyes like diamonds against his tanned skin. *"I know, little buddy."*

"Will you marry me when I grow up?"

At this point Skye woke abruptly. It was then the tears came.

CHAPTER ONE

FOLLOWING instructions, she took a domestic flight to Longreach, where she was to be met by Scott who would fly her back to the station. She was none too happy about that. She hadn't forgiven Scott. And she had tried.

The news of Broderick McGovern's death had been broken to her by her father, who had worshipped the man. A short time later the news broke on radio, T.V. and the Internet. Broderick McGovern, billionaire "Cattle King", had been killed in a helicopter crash while being ferried to a McGovern outstation on the border of the Northern Territory. He, the pilot and another passenger, a relative and federal politician, had been killed when the helicopter, flown by an experienced pilot, simply "fell out of the sky", according to a lone witness who had been rounding up brumbies at the time.

No one had been prepared for this violent assault by Fate.

Keefe McGovern, 30, Broderick McGovern's elder son, was now master of Djinjara, the historic Outback station. Mr McGovern could not be reached for comment. The family was said to be in total shock. Broderick McGovern had only been 55 years of age.

Such had been his stature, not only as one of the country's richest men, a philanthropist and premier cattle producer, that the Prime Minister announced with genuine regret, *"This is a man who will be sorely missed."*

Skye stood under a broad awning, waiting for Scott to arrive. Scott was another one who had a hold on her memory. She wondered if he had matured at all since she had last seen him; wondered if his fierce jealousy of his older brother had abated over time. Both Scott and Rachelle were very much affected by having a brother like Keefe. Instead of making their own mark, they chose to remain in Keefe's long shadow. Scott, who had been trained in the cattle business and played an active role, sadly lacked Keefe's extraordinary level of competence, let alone the leadership qualities necessary in a man who had to run a huge man-orientated enterprise. Still he raged, secretly secure in the knowledge he would in all probability never be called upon. Rachelle, the heiress daughter, made no effort at all to find her own niche in the world. She preferred to live on Djinjara and take numerous holidays at home and abroad whenever she found herself bored.

To Skye it was an empty, aimless life. She had no idea what would have happened had Scott been his father's heir instead of Keefe. Instead, Scott and Rachelle acted as if their lives had been mapped out for them.

Goodness, it was hot! Far, far hotter than it ever was in sub-tropical Brisbane, but this was the dry heat of the Outback. Oddly its effects on her were invigorating. She had grown up in heat like this. Even the slight breeze was bringing in the familiar, tantalising scent of the bush. She drew in a breath of the aromatic fragrance, trying to calm herself and unravel the tight knots in her stomach. It wasn't easy, returning to Djinjara, but it was unthinkable not to attend Broderick McGovern's funeral. He had always been kind to her and to her father, who was in genuine mourning.

It wasn't the time to wish it was Keefe who was coming for her. She knew perfectly well Keefe wouldn't be able to get away. He had taken on his dead father's mantle. But she still had many reservations about Scott. He had always been a chameleon when they had been growing up. Sometimes he had been fun, if a bit wild, other times a darkness had descended on him. He idolised his brother. No question. But to Scott's own dismay he'd had to constantly battle a sometimes overwhelming jealousy of Keefe, the heir. It had made him angry and resentful, ready to lash out at everyone on the station who couldn't answer back without the possible risk of getting fired. That included her father who felt pity for Scott McGovern, the classic second string with all its attendant problems.

When Scott was in his moods, especially as he grew older, station people learned to steer clear of him until the mood passed. Skye in later years realised she was perhaps the only one who had missed out for the most part on Scott's sharp, hurtful ways. It had taken a while for her to become aware that Keefe had always appeared to keep a pretty close eye on them.

Why?

She had found out. And a lot sooner than she had ever imagined. When she had been around sixteen and Scott almost twenty he had fancied himself either in love with her or determined to take advantage of her. Either way, it was the cause of an ongoing simmering tension between the two brothers. One that stemmed from a single violent confrontation.

Over her.

All these years later, Skye remembered that traumatic episode as though it were yesterday…

As she stepped into the deep emerald lagoon, catching her breath at its coldness, Skye became aware someone was watching her. She spun about, calling, "Who's there?"

She wasn't nervous. She felt perfectly safe anywhere on the station. She knew everyone and everyone knew her. There wasn't a soul on the station who hadn't kept an eye on her as she was growing up. They had all known her beautiful mother. They worked alongside her father. The entire station community had as good as adopted her. No one would harm her. She called again, startling a flock of sulphur-crested, white cockatoos that set up a noisy protest. A few seconds later, lanky Scott appeared. He had the McGovern height but not Keefe's great shape. He was dressed in his everyday working gear—skintight jeans, checked cotton shirt, riding boots. His hat was tipped down over his face. He had the McGovern widow's peak that looked so dramatic on his older brother but vaguely sinister on him.

"Why didn't you speak?" she asked in surprise. How long had he been watching her from the cover of the tree—three minutes, four? She had stripped down to her turquoise and white bikini, leaving her clothes neatly folded on the sand.

He didn't move. Didn't respond. He remained where he was at the top of the sloping bank, the loose sand bound by a profusion of hardy succulent-type plants with pockets of tiny perfumed white and mauve lilies in between.

"Scott?" she questioned, shading her eyes with her hand. "Is something wrong?"

Suddenly he smiled, spread out his long arms, then half ran, half skidded, like they had done when they had been kids, down the bank to the golden crescent of sand. "Boy, oh, boy, you should get a look at yourself," he whooped. "That's some bikini, girl!"

It wasn't the words, normal enough, but the way he said them that caused her first ever flurry of unease. "Like it?" She answered in a deliberately casual voice, nothing that could remotely sound like a come-on in her tone. "It's new." This was Scott. This was a McGovern. Much was expected of them.

"You have a beautiful body, Skye, baby," he drawled, his eyes moving very slowly and insolently over her. "Beautiful face. That blonde mane of hair and those sparkly blue eyes!"

He moved closer, tossing his wide-brimmed hat away. "I'm coming in."

She wanted to shout, No! Some expression on his face was causing her alarm. Instead she managed, "Don't, Scott."

For answer he began to strip off his shirt. "Don't tell me what I can and can't do, Skye McCory."

It sounded remarkably like a threat. That put the fight into her. "Well, you'll have to swim alone," she announced crisply. "I'm coming out. I have things to do."

"What things?" He spoke disparagingly, sounding a bit too much like his sister for comfort. "Don't try to disappear on me," he warned.

Now he was stripping off his jeans.

A voice inside told her things had changed. In his briefs, she couldn't avoid seeing he was sexually aroused. Immediately she decided to change tack and strike out for the opposite bank. What then? She was a good swimmer with a lot of pace. Scott was coming after her. What was his plan, to trap her? Not only cold water washed over her. She felt the icy finger of panic. She couldn't help knowing males got intense pleasure from looking at her these days. Even her friends at boarding school teased her all the time about the crushes their brothers had on her.

She reached the jade shallows, pulling herself up out of the water, her heart banging against her ribs. Swiftly she shook back her long hair. It had come free of its plait. Where to now? Take one of the trails?

Scott pulled himself out of the water seconds after her, his grin tight. "What's the matter with you?" he challenged.

She put her arms around herself, shielding her small breasts, their contours enhanced by the snugly fitting bra top from his view. "What's the matter with you is more to the point?" she said sharply. "You're upsetting me, Scott." Indeed, he was changing her perception of him.

His answer was to lurch towards her, fixing her with a look that dismayed her. He easily pinned her wrists, because he was very much taller and stronger. "I want to kiss you. I want you to kiss me back."

Part of her brain searched for words to stop him but couldn't find them. He was overstepping the boundaries and he knew it. "Are you mad?" She got ready to aim a well-deserved kick at his groin. She was an Outback-bred girl. She knew all the ways a lone woman could defend herself.

"Mad for you." There was the fierce glow of lust in his eyes.

She looked around her quickly. On this side of the lagoon the trees grew more thickly. There was sunlight coming in streams through the canopy, lighting up the trails taken by horses and riders. This particular lagoon was her favourite swimming spot, one of many on the vast station, but today the whole magnificent wild area seemed threatening and deserted. "Take a deep breath, Scott," she cautioned, wishing Keefe would miraculously ride that way. "Stop this now."

"Stop what?" He leaned closer to her.

"What you think you've started. It's not on. So get yourself together. Remember who you are."

Scott set his jaw, his handsome face turning grim. "I'm not Keefe. Is that it? I'll never be Keefe. Keefe is the one you want." His grip on her wrists became punishingly hard as his pathological jealousy grew.

She responded with heat. "You're hurting me, Scott." She wasn't about to show her fear. She stood her ground, even if inwardly she cringed.

Abruptly he released her, but just as she relaxed, one of his hands reached out to caress her breast. He wasn't toying with her. He was dead serious.

She flung herself backwards and dashed a tear from her eye. Surely she wasn't crying? She never cried. A small fallen branch lay on the sand. She bent sideways to pick it up. If she had to defend herself, she would. She knew with Scott in this mood something bad could happen to her.

He found it too easy to create fear in her. Scott appeared to be enjoying her efforts at evasion. "Give up," he advised with a brittle laugh. "I'm really mad about you, Skye. That's what I'm tryin' to tell you. Don't you care?"

There was a hard knot at the base of her breastbone. "I care that you're making a huge mistake, Scott." Her voice was tight with strain. "You're my friend. You're Scott. You can't be anything more to me."

He struck like lightning. She landed a stinging lash on his arm. The tanned skin reddened immediately but he didn't look at the welt, or appear to feel it. No matter how much she wished otherwise, there was no mistaking her imminent danger and his raw intent. Scott meant to have his way. Kiss her? Or take her forcibly? Anything was possible. Who was she to him anyway? Only the overseer's daughter. Dozens of girls would gladly have swapped places with her, no matter the risk. Scott McGovern mightn't be his brother, but he was still a great catch.

"Now, what makes you think that?" he asked with slow menace. "I tell you, Skye, you've turned into the sexiest thing on two legs."

I'm scared but I can't show it.

Find me, Keefe. Find me.

She concentrated on sending her message out into the great plains. "This isn't going to work, Scott. You'd better find someone else."

"I don't want anyone else." He cut her off with a chopping motion of his hand. "And when I make up my mind, I don't change it."

"Then go to hell!" she shouted, adrenalin flooding into her blood. "You're acting like a bully and a coward."

It was a mistake.

Scott reached for her, wrapping one arm around her. "This can work, Skye if you let it."

"No. No. And no!" She fought back, digging in her nails.

"Too ordinary for you, am I? I'm not Keefe."

She threw back her head. "Keefe would never force a woman," she cried with utter conviction.

"Wouldn't have to, would he? You'd let him take you in a minute!" There was rage and bitter resentment in Scott's blue eyes as he repeated his resentment of his older brother. He went to kiss her and she turned her face, both of them recoiling abruptly as a familiar voice came from behind them in a barely contained roar of ferocity.

"What the hell is going on here?"

Keefe's tall, wide-shouldered, lean figure came stalking along the narrow sunlit corridor. His body language was wrathful. He looked blazingly angry, angrier than Skye could ever have imagined. Keefe was famous for keeping his cool.

Now it was Scott's turn to be intimidated. Instead of attempting an answer, he appeared ludicrously shocked, while Skye found herself moaning her relief. With no thought to her actions, she ran to Keefe's side, grasping his hard, muscled arm, feeling the heat of rage sizzle off his skin.

"Okay, I guess I know what was happening," he rasped, shoving Skye bodily behind him. "You can't help yourself, can you, Scott? The only thing that concerns you is getting what you want."

"And I would have got it if you hadn't turned up. Skye has the hots for me."

"Believe that, and you'll believe anything," Keefe bit off with disgust. He closed the short distance to where his brother stood, grabbing hold of his bare shoulder with such force Scott winced. "Goddammit, Scott," Keefe groaned in a kind of agony. "I'm repulsed by you. Where's your sense of decency? Your sense of honour?

"You got the lot," Scott retorted with sudden venom, trying unsuccessfully to break his brother's iron grasp. "You want her yourself."

Keefe's expression was daunting. "What you're saying is what I want, you must take for yourself."

"Well, she is one alluring little chick!"

That was when Keefe hit him. Scott dropped to the sand with blood streaming from his nose. He tried to get up, fell back again, moaning. "Can't say I didn't have that coming," he wailed, as unpredictable as ever.

"You bastard!" Keefe raged with a mix of horror and regret. "You never can deal with the consequences of your actions. Why do you let your dark side take you under?'

Skye, who had been frozen to the spot, now rushed to Keefe's side. She had to make an attempt to allay his rage. "Don't hit him again, Keefe. Please. Nothing happened."

"Keep out of this," Keefe warned, with the blackest of frowns. "Get dressed and go home."

His anger sparked an answering anger in Skye. "Don't treat me like a child."

He turned on her, his silver-grey eyes so brilliant they bored right into her. "A child?" he ground out. "You're no longer a child, Skye. You're a woman, with all a woman's power. My brother isn't such a monster."

"She's temptation on legs," Scott offered from his prone position on the sand. To his mind that exonerated him from all blame.

"Shut up!" Keefe violently kicked up the sand near him. "Apologise to Skye. Tell her you were acting crazy. Tell her such a thing will never happen again. And it won't, believe me. This is your one and only warning. You'll have me to deal with."

Scott wilted beneath his brother's fury and disgust. "You won't tell Dad," he choked, his hand pressed to his bleeding nose.

"Dad?" Keefe roared. *"Apologise to Skye. How could you begin to betray her trust?"*

Shaking all over, Skye fervently wished for her clothes, which were lying in a tidy pile on the opposite bank. As it was, she had to stand there, receiving the attention she didn't want. Her brief bikini barely covered her. Even now she couldn't believe what Scott had done. A woman's beauty came with inherent dangers. Beauty brought fixations and unwelcome attention. The last thing in the world she wanted was to rouse the brute in a man. Now Scott! She had never dreamed she would be in this position, coming between the two brothers. She was the innocent party here, yet Keefe appeared to be so furious with her she might as well have been as guilty of wrongdoing as Scott.

Scott took the opportunity to stagger to his feet, gingerly feeling his jaw. Pain lanced up into his head. "I'm sorry, Skye," he mumbled. "You know a lot about me so you know from time to time I run off the rails. I would never hurt you. I just wanted a kiss."

"A kiss and the rest!" Keefe shouted, hooked into his rage.

"You sure pack a punch, Keefe. You really hurt me." Unbelievably Scott appeared to be feeling sorry for himself.

"You're lucky I didn't pummel you into the ground," Keefe cried.

"Damn! Damn everything," Scott moaned. "So what am I supposed to do now, avoid her?"

"What you're supposed to do is what you've been reared to do. Treat Skye—all women—with respect. You think Dad would be angry? What about Gran? She'd have you horsewhipped."

"She would, too." Scott suddenly grinned.

"Oh, please, please, stop," Skye begged.

Only then did Keefe turn to stare at her. "Are you okay?"

She was caught in that diamond-hard star, so fierce she almost felt terror. "I told you. He didn't touch me." All she wanted was for this dreadful episode to be over.

Keefe's laugh was a rasp. "Only because I turned up. I'll never know why I came this way. I thought I heard you calling me."

She had been.

The part of him beyond reason had clearly heard her.

A few minutes elapsed before a small airport runabout swept into sight. It pulled up beside her and the driver got out, coming around the rear of the vehicle. Skye gave a convulsive gasp. Some emotions were so extreme they couldn't be put to rest.

Keefe.

The world she had tried hard to build up for herself started to disintegrate and turn to rubble.

All you've got to do is breathe in and breathe out. Breathe in. Breathe out.

It was the voice of reason, only it took several seconds before she could even swallow. Inside she felt a piercing thrill of the old excitement. Outside a near-paralysis. Focusing hard, she drew a deep calming breath into her lungs. It didn't quell the clamour. Her nerves were bunched tight. How did she hide her enormous vulnerability when it was pitted against a towering wave of pleasure?

He was even more handsome in maturity, but harder, tougher, severe of expression. All traces of that wonderful tenderness had gone. Some might say his arresting good looks were a bit on the intimidating side, given the air of gravitas and authority he projected. She knew strangers had sometimes mistaken that aura for arrogance. They were wrong. It was Keefe's heightened sense of responsibility, of being who he was, instilled in him from childhood. He looked stunningly fit from a lifetime of hard physical activity. His darkly tanned skin glowed richly. His thickly curling sable hair worn longer than was usual—hairdressers were few and far between in the bush—was swept back from his forehead in the manner of some medieval prince. Strong and distinctive as his features were, they were dominated by his remarkable wide-set eyes. They were a mesmerising silver-grey, brilliant, crystal clear, yet impossible to read.

He didn't smile. Neither did she.

The air crackled as it did when an electrical storm approached. They stood there studying one another in silence. Skye felt a deep, sharp sadness. As for Keefe, she couldn't read him. As in everything, for so long now, he was an enigma. He had distanced himself from her as she had distanced herself from him. But what did he *really* want of her? What did she want of him? What were the changes each one of them saw in the other? She was ill prepared for this confrontation. Had she known Keefe was to come for her, she could have worked on some defence strategy.

Don't kid yourself, girl. Such a strategy doesn't exist.

There was always drama around the McGoverns. Instead of Scott, Keefe had appeared. The man she dreamed about, so often and so vividly, that it was as if he was in bed with her. He was dressed in a khaki bush shirt with epaulettes and buttoned-down pockets, close-fitting jeans, beaten-copper-buckled leather belt, glossy riding boots on his feet. Everyday wear, but quality all the way. There was something utterly compelling about a splendid male body, she thought raggedly, the height, the width of shoulder, the narrowness of waist and hip descending into long, long straight legs.

"It's good to see you, Skye." Finally he spoke. "Weren't waiting long?"

She readied herself. His voice, like the rest of him, carried a natural command. It had become more and more like his father's; the timbre deep and dark, the accent polished and slightly clipped. "No more than five minutes," she said with admirable composure. She had to force the adrenalin rush down. "I wasn't expecting you, Keefe. I was told Scott was coming."

"Well, *I'm* here," he said, looking directly into her eyes.

He was so beautiful! All strength and sinew with an intense sexual aura. Her entire body leapt to vivid life, sparks coursing like little fires along her veins. What she felt for Keefe couldn't be easily governed. Even her nerves were like tightly strung wires humming and vibrating inside her. How long had it been since she had felt this mad surge of excitement? Not since the last time she had been with him. Years of loving Keefe. Years of unfinished business. It was like they were tied together against their wills. She pulled in a deep breath, keeping her tone neutral.

"And thank you. I appreciate it." No way could she betray the tumult in her heart. "I'm so very sorry about your father, Keefe. I know how hard it must be for you."

His glittering gaze moved to the middle distance. "Forgive me, Skye. I can't talk about it."

"Of course not. I understand."

"You always did have more sensitivity than anyone else," he commented briefly, reaching for her suitcase. It was heavy—she had packed too much into just one case—but he lifted it as though its weight were negligible. "We'd best get away. As you can imagine, there's much to be done at home."

She shook her head helplessly. "You didn't *have* to come for me, Keefe."

He paused to give her another searing glance. "I *did*."

Ah, the heady magnetism of his gaze! She moved quickly, letting her honey-blonde hair cascade across one side of her face. Anything to hide the wild hot rush of blood. She opened the passenger door, then slid into the seat. All the years she had spent mounting defences against Keefe…!

You still have no protection.

Their flight into Djinjara couldn't have been smoother. Keefe was an experienced pilot. But, then, his skills were many, all burnished to a high polish. He had been groomed from child-hood to take over leadership from his father.

They were *home*.

Djinjara was still—would always be—the best place in the world. The vastness, the freedom, the call of the wild. There was a magic to it she had never found in the city, for all the glamour of her hectic life there. She had made many friends. Some of them in high places. She was asked every-where. She had a stack of admirers. She knew she was rated a fine, committed advocate. Her clients trusted her, looked to her to get them through their difficult times. Her career was on the up and up. Yet, oddly, though she had hoped to gain great satisfaction from it all, that hadn't happened. Sometimes she felt disconnected from her city life. Other times she felt disconnected from everything. Successful on the outside, when she allowed herself time for introspection, she felt curiously *empty*. Starved of what she really wanted.

Such was the pull of love; the elation, the sense of com-pletion in being with Keefe. But along with it went long periods of *loneliness*.

On the ground, beneath a deliriously blue sky, she marked the familiar spectacular flights of birds, the shadows beneath the rolling red sand dunes that stretched across the vast plains. The sands were heavily embossed with huge pincushions of spinifex scorched to a dark gold; in the shimmering distance the purple of the eroded hills with their caves and secret, crystal-clear waterholes.

Skye drew the unique pungent aromas of the bush into her lungs, realising how much she had missed Djinjara. The mingling wind-whipped scents, so aromatic like crushed and dried native herbs, to her epitomised the Outback. She had a very real feel for the place of her birth, even though her mother had died here giving her life. Not everyone fell under the spell of the bush but Djinjara, from her earliest memories, had held her captive.

They were met by her father. He had been lolling against a station Jeep, a tall whipcord-thin man with a lived-in, interesting sort of face and love for his daughter shining out of bright blue eyes.

"Skye, darling girl! It's marvellous to see you." Jack rushed forward, his hard muscled arms wide stretched in greeting.

"Marvellous to see *you*, Dad." Skye picked up her own pace, meeting up with her father joyously. She went into his embrace, kissing his weathered mahogany cheek. He smelled of sunlight, leather and horses. "I've missed you *so* much."

"Missed you." Jack looked down into his daughter's beautiful face, revelling in her presence, the glorious grace of her. She was so like his beloved Cathy. The way she smiled. The way she *shone*.

"Sad about Mr McGovern," Skye spoke in a low voice.

"Tragic!" her father agreed, dropping his arms as Keefe, who had given father and daughter a few moments alone, came towards them.

Keefe was a stunning-looking man by any standard, Skye thought. Quite unlike any other man she had ever seen. "I'll take you up to the house first, boss," Jack called. "Then I'll drop Skye off."

"Fine," Keefe responded. The force field around him was such it drew father and daughter in. "I know you'll want to spend this first night together, Jack. You must have much to catch up on—but I thought as the bungalow is on the small side, Skye might be more comfortable up at the house for the rest of her stay." He looked from one to the other. "It's entirely up to you."

Skye's heart leapt, then dropped like a stone. She had no stomach for the rest of the family, other than Lady McGovern.

"I'll stay with Dad," she answered promptly, "but thank you for the kind thought, Keefe." Despite herself, a certain dryness crept into her tone.

"You might want to change your mind, my darling," Jack said wryly, looking at his beautiful daughter. He was immensely gratified she wanted to stay with him, but worried the bungalow really *was* too small.

"Well, see how it goes," Keefe clipped off.

"It's very good of you, Keefe." Jack looked respectfully towards the younger man.

"Not at all." Keefe turned his splendid profile. "My grandmother will want to see you, Skye."

"Of course." She couldn't miss out on an audience with Lady McGovern, who would be devastated by the loss of her son. Pity rushed in. Besides, she could never forget what she owed the McGoverns for what they had done for her. Albeit without her knowledge.

Jack watched on, sensing an odd tension between the boss and his daughter. It hadn't always been like that. Skye had adored Keefe all the time she had been growing up. Keefe had been there for her, like an affectionate and protective big brother. It was only half a joke, suggesting Skye might change her mind. His beautiful girl, his princess, belonged in a palace, not a bungalow. Keefe was right. The bungalow wasn't a fitting place for her now she had grown into a lovely accomplished woman. A lawyer no less! At home in her city world. His Skye, far more than the caustic Rachelle, the McGovern heiress, looked and acted the part, Jack thought with pride. Skye's beauty and her gifts came from her mother. They certainly didn't come from him. He was just an ordinary bloke. He still couldn't believe Cathy, who had come into his life as Lady McGovern's young visitor, had fallen in love with him and, miracle of miracles, agreed to marry him. It had been like a fairy-tale. But, like many a fairy-tale, it had had a tragic end.

CHAPTER TWO

GRIEF was contagious. The faces of the hundreds of mourners who attended Broderick McGovern's Outback funeral showed genuine sadness and a communal sense of loss. There was no trace of mixed emotions anywhere. This was a sad, sad day. He had been a man of power and influence, but incredibly he had gone through life without attracting enemies. The overriding reason had to be that he had been a just man, egalitarian in his dealings; a man who had never wronged anyone and had never been known to go back on his word. Broderick McGovern had been a gentleman in the finest sense of the word.

All the men and most of the women, except for the elderly and the handful of young women who were pregnant, had elected to make the long walk from the homestead to the McGovern graveyard set down in the shadow of a strange fiery red sandstone monolith rising some hundred feet above the great spinifex plain. The McGovern family from the earliest days of settlement had called it Manguri, after one of the tribal gods. The great sandstone pillar did, in fact, bear a remarkable resemblance to a totem figure, only Manguri was the last remaining vestige of a table-topped mountain of pre-history.

Like all the desert monoliths, Manguri had the capacity to change colour through the day, from the range of pinks commencing at dawn, to the fiery reds of noon, to the mauves and the amethysts of evening. It was a fascinating phenomenon. Generations of McGoverns had been buried in Manguri's shadow. Curiously, Skye's own mother was buried in an outlying plot when the custom was for station employees right from the early days to be buried at another well-tended graveyard. In the old days there had been some talk of Cathy being distantly related to Lady McGovern. The rumour had never been confirmed. Certainly not by the McGoverns. As a lawyer, Skye could have checked out her mother's background had she so chosen. Instead, she found herself making the conscious decision *not* to investigate her mother's past. She didn't know why, exactly, beyond a powerful gut feeling. Was she frightened of what she might find? She would admit only to an instinctive unease. Her father had always said her mother had been an orphan Lady McGovern had taken an interest in. Much like her own case.

She wasn't the only young person on the station the McGoverns had sent on to tertiary education either. Most of the sons and daughters of station employees elected to live and work on Djinjara. It was home to them. They loved it and the way of life. But others, of recent times, all young men of exceptional academic ability, had been sent on to university by the McGoverns. One was a doctor in charge of a bush hospital. The others were engineers working in the great minefields of Western Australia.

All three were present today.

Keefe had made it perfectly plain she was expected to come up to the house afterwards, even if her father was not. Jack held an important position as overseer but he knew and accepted his place in the social scheme of things. It was the last thing Skye wanted to do, but her father had urged her and she was painfully aware of her obligations. The scores of ordinary folk who had made the long hot overland trek in a convoy of vehicles were being catered for in huge marquees set up within the extensive grounds of the home compound. The more important folk, the entire McGovern clan, fellow cattle barons and pastoralists along with their families, and a large contingent of VIPs crowded their way into Djinjara's splendid homestead, which had grown over the years since the 1860s when Malcolm James McGovern, a Scottish adventurer of good family, had established his kingdom in the wilds. Oddly, Djinjara with its fifty rooms looked more like an English country mansion that anything else, but Malcolm was said to have greatly admired English architecture and customs and had kept up his close ties with his mother's English family. The bonds remained in place to the present day. Lady McGovern was English, and a distant relative. She had come to Australia, a world far removed from her own, as Kenneth McGovern's—later Sir Kenneth McGovern—bride. In her new home, despite all the odds, she had thrived. And, it had to be said, *ruled.*

Try as she did to move inconspicuously about the large reception rooms and the magnificent double-height library, Skye was uncomfortably aware that a great many people were looking at her. Staring really. She had to contend with the fact she would never melt into a crowd. Not with the looks she had inherited from her mother. Some people she recognised from her childhood but she wasn't sure if they recognised her. Others acknowledged her with genuine warmth and kindly expressed admiration for her achievements. She was dressed in traditional black but she couldn't help knowing black suited her blonde colouring. She had discarded the wide-brimmed black hat that had protected her face and neck from the blazing sun, but she still wore her hair in a classic French pleat. As a hairstyle it looked very elegant, but the pins were making her head ache.

She had sighted Scott with a dark-haired young woman

always at his side. She was rather plain of face, conservative in her dress for her age—the black dress was slightly too large for her—but she had a look of intelligence and breeding that saved the day. Jemma Templeton of Cudgee Downs. Skye hadn't seen her for a few years but she was aware Jemma had always had a crush on Scott. Rachelle, stick thin, fine boned and patrician-looking—the McGoverns were a very good-looking family—kept herself busy moving from group to group, carrying her responsibilities, it could be said, to the extremes. Rachelle was more about form than feeling. Doing what was expected. The show of manners. She had never shown any to the young Skye. Skye knew Rachelle had spotted her but had determined on not saying hello unless forced into it. Rachelle didn't have *friends*—hadn't even at school. As a McGovern she only had minions.

I bring out the worst in her, Skye thought regretfully. And there's nothing I can do about it. Rachelle will never make peace with me. She resents me bitterly. And it's all about Keefe.

She turned away just as a rather dashing young man with close-cropped fair hair rushed to stand directly in front of her, obscuring her view. "Skye, it is you, isn't it?" he burst out with enthusiasm. "Of course it is! Mum said it was. That blonde hair and those blue eyes! You're an absolute knockout!"

Skye had to smile at such enthusiasm. "Why thank you, Robert." Robert Sullivan was one of the McGovern clan, the grandson of one of Broderick McGovern's sisters. He had had three. There had been a younger brother too. But he had died tragically when he had crashed his motorbike on the station when he was only in his early twenties. "You look well yourself. It's been a long time." The last time she had seen Robert had been at a McGovern family Christmas Eve party some years back.

"Too long." He gave an exaggerated moan. "I say, why don't you come and sit with me? I'll find somewhere quiet.

Look at this lot!" His hazel glance swept the room. "They're knocking back food and drink like it was a party. Terrible about Uncle Brod."

"Indeed it is," Skye lamented. "He always seemed so indestructible. The family will miss him greatly." She broke off as her eyes fell on Lady McGovern, who was seated in an antique giltwood high-backed chair not unlike a throne. She was indicating with a slight movement of her hand that she wanted Skye to come over. "Rob, would you excuse me one moment?" she said, placing a hand on Robert's jacket sleeve. "Lady McGovern is beckoning me. I haven't had a chance to offer my condolences as yet."

"Tough old bird," Robert murmured, with not a lot of liking but definite respect. "Not a tear out of her. Stiff upper lip. Straight back. Father was a general, don't you know?"

"Yes, I do," Skye answered a trifle sharply. Robert's words had annoyed her. "Because Lady McGovern doesn't cry in public, it doesn't mean she's not crying inside, Robert. I know she will be grief stricken even if it's her way not to show it."

"Okay, okay." Robert held up placating hands. "Training and all that. She's always made me feel as though I'm not quite up to scratch. Of course, no one *could* be beside Keefe. Come back to me when you've finished paying your respects. I want to hear all about what you've been doing, you clever girl! Mother is very impressed. She spotted you the instant you walked into the room. You *do* stand out. 'Why, that's little Skye McCory all grown up! And she looks simply stunning! One would never know she had such a humble start.'"

Skye hadn't forgotten how patronising the McGoverns were.

"There you are, my dear," Lady McGovern said, indicating with her heavily be-ringed hand an empty chair beside her. Lady Margaret McGovern was a diminutive woman but she had enormous presence. Even at eighty it was easy to see she once had been a beauty. The bone structure was still there. Her skin stretched very tight over those bones was remarkably soft and unlined.

Skye obeyed. "I'm so very sorry, Lady McGovern," she murmured as she sat down. "I couldn't get to you before with so many people wanting to offer their condolences. I know how much pain you're in. I feel so sad myself. Mr McGovern was a wonderful man. He was always very kind to me."

"Who could not be?" Lady McGovern said. She took Skye's two hands in her own, her face carefully in control of emotions. "Welcome home, Skye."

It was so unexpected, so enormously comforting, that tears sprang to Skye's eyes. *Home?* With an effort of will she forced the tears away. Too many people were watching.

"Let me look at you," Lady McGovern said, turning her full scrutiny on Skye. "You're even more beautiful than your mother. But the colour of your hair is *exactly* the same. The same radiant blue eyes full of expression. She would have been very proud of you."

"Oh, I hope so!" Skye released a fluttery breath. "But I wouldn't be where I am today without *you*, Lady McGovern. I will never forget that."

"Enough of the Lady McGovern!" The old lady spoke as if she were heartily sick of the title. "I want you to call me Margaret, or Lady Margaret if you feel more comfortable with that. Margaret is my name. It's a name long in my own family. I would like you to use it. I rarely hear it any more. It's Gran and Nan, Aunt and Great-Aunt and, I dare say, the Old Dragon. Don't try to tell me you can't do it. I look on you as family, Skye."

That touched a finger to an open wound. Some things would seem to be hidden, but they couldn't be hidden for ever. "I've always felt something of it," she confessed. "But why? Can't you tell me?" The plea came straight from the heart.

"Who *was* my mother really? I never knew her, which is the tragedy of my life. Dad always said she was an orphan." Skye's frown deepened. "He said she spoke beautifully. Not an educated Australian accent, but an English voice. Like you. Was she English?" There was something in Lady McGovern's fine dark eyes that was making Skye very uneasy.

"As a solicitor, Skye, you've made no attempt to trace your mother's background?" Lady McGovern asked with a grim smile. Could it be pain or disapproval?

"Very oddly, *no,* Lady Margaret." Now that she had said it, "Lady Margaret" came surprisingly easily to her tongue.

"You had concerns about what you might find?" Again the piercing regard.

Skye shook her head. "After all, my mother had a connection to you." Though she didn't expect to be answered, Skye prepared herself for whatever might come.

In vain. "I was very fond of her," Lady McGovern said briefly, then changed the subject. "Your use of my name comes sweetly to my ear. Kindly continue to use it, no matter what. I'm fully aware my granddaughter has always been jealous of you. Jealous of Keefe's affection for you. That is her nature. She's going to find it very hard to find a husband if she's expecting someone like Keefe to come along. It won't happen."

"No," Skye agreed quietly. "Rachelle loves both her brothers, but she adores Keefe."

"Exactly." Lady McGovern brushed the topic aside. "I want you to know Cathy herself chose your father."

"But of course!" Skye was startled. "She fell in love with him." She knew she was supposed to hold her tongue but it got away from her. "But how did they find the opportunities to meet? She stayed at the house on her visits. My father at the time was a stockman. Times have changed somewhat, but there was a huge social divide."

"Of course," Lady McGovern acknowledged, as if the

divide was still firmly in place. "Nevertheless, Cathy knew Jack McCory was the man for her. And a fine man he is too. He mourns your mother to this day. As do I. Let's not talk any more about this, Skye. It upsets me. I don't know if Jack ever told you, but Cathy knew the baby she was carrying was a girl. She had the name Skye already picked out for you. And doesn't it suit you! Somehow she knew you would have her beautiful sky-blue eyes."

Skye stayed a few minutes more talking to Lady McGovern, but it was obvious others wanted the opportunity to express a few words of sympathy to the McGovern matriarch. She no sooner moved away than Robert Sullivan made a bee-line to her side.

"I don't really know why but you and my great-aunt look more comfortable together than she and Rachelle," he announced. "Why is that, do you suppose?"

"I have no idea, Robert," she responded calmly.

"Neither do I. Just one of those quirky things." Robert took her arm and began to lead her away. "Look, how long are you staying?" He stared down at her smooth honey-blonde head.

"No more than a week." Actually, she had weeks of her leave left. "I only came for the funeral."

"But we've got to meet up." Robert spoke with extraordinary determination. "I've thought of asking Keefe if I can spend a little time here. I'm sure he won't mind. The house is big enough to billet an army."

"But won't you be expected back home?" Robert worked for his father, a well-known pastoralist running both sheep and cattle on a large property on the Queensland/New South Wales border.

"I could do with a break. I'll check it out with Dad. He was as impressed with you as Mother. I want you to come over and say hello. That's if I can find them in this crush. Even in this huge house there's hardly room to move. And just look at Keefe!"

Look at him! Skye couldn't drag her eyes off him. Everything about him pierced her to the heart.

"The minute he enters the room, he's the stand-out figure," Robert said with undisguised envy. "And it's not just his height. He really takes the eye. He's a man with power. And money. Poor old Scott is still as jealous of him as he ever was. Scott really ought to go away and make a life for himself. Rachelle, too, though she spends plenty of time in Sydney and Melbourne."

"I see Scott with Jemma Templeton," Skye sidetracked. She didn't want to discuss Rachelle. "What I remember of Jemma is good."

"But isn't she plain?" Robert groaned, with a pitying look in his eyes. "Talk about a face like a horse!"

"A particularly well-bred one." Skye's eyes were still on Keefe's tall, commanding figure. He looked beyond handsome in his formal funeral attire. "I don't consider Jemma plain at all. She has a look of breeding and intelligence.'

"I suppose. But I bet she'd love to be pretty. And you *are* being kind. I suppose a woman as beautiful as you can afford to be kind. Poor old Jemma must be nuts if she's looking to land Scott. She's mad about him, poor thing!" Robert rushed on with characteristic candour. "Who knows why. Doesn't say much for her intelligence in my book. Scott is trouble. It's the way he goes off like an out-of-control rocket from time to time."

"Whatever, he's always got a whole string of girls after him."

"And Keefe?" Couldn't she control her tongue?

Robert didn't appear to notice the tautness of her tone. "Who knows what's on Keefe's mind?" he mused. "A couple of stayers are hanging in there. Fiona Fraser and Clemmie Cartwright. You remember them. My money's on Fiona. She's swanning around somewhere. She's stylish, well connected, knows the score, sharp as a tack but beneath that she's the worst of things—a snob."

"And you're not?" Skye gave him a sweetly sarcastic smile.

"Of course I'm not!" He denied the charge. "Mum is, maybe. Clemmie is nicer, totally different, but I don't believe she can fit the bill.'

"Surely it's all up to Keefe?"

"Maybe he hasn't found the woman to measure up?" Robert pondered. "He's a great guy, don't get me wrong. I admire him enormously. I'm not in his league. None of us are, for that matter. The guy's a prince!"

He's always been a prince. My prince.

By late afternoon everyone, with the exception of a few relatives who were staying overnight, had made their way home in the private planes and the charter planes that had been dotted all over the airfield, the half-dozen helicopters, bright yellow like bumblebees, and the convoys of vehicles that would make the return journey overland. Skye, who had returned to Lady McGovern's side as requested, found herself one of the last to leave. She had made her way to the entrance hall when Rachelle suddenly confronted her, a smile on her lips, her eyes cold and flat.

"So, Skye! Sorry I didn't get a minute to speak to you earlier. How are you?"

"I'm well, thank you, Rachelle." Skye spoke gently. "Please accept my condolences. The manner of your father's premature death was terrible. I know you will miss him greatly."

"Of course. He was a great man," Rachelle said stiffly. "How long exactly are you staying?" As usual she was talking down to Skye.

"A few days."

"I'm sure Gran asked you to come up to the house," Rachelle challenged. "To stay, I mean."

"Both Lady Margaret and Keefe invited me but I'm quite happy staying with my father. I won't get in your way, Rachelle, if that's what's bothering you."

Rachelle's face took on an expression of extreme hauteur. "You couldn't bother me if you tried. And I certainly don't like the way you refer to my grandmother as Lady Margaret. She's Lady McGovern to you."

"Why don't you check with your grandmother?" Skye said quietly, preparing to move on. "It was she who asked me to call her that."

Rachelle's dark eyes held a wild glare. "I don't believe you."

Skye ignored her, continuing on her way. On this day of days Rachelle, incredibly, was looking for a fight.

She hadn't been at the bungalow ten minutes before she heard footsteps resounding on the short flight of timber stairs. They didn't sound like her father's. Not at all. They sounded like… She hurried to the front door, gripped by tension. The door wasn't shut. She had left it open to catch a breeze. The bungalow had ceiling fans, but no air-conditioning.

To her complete shock, Keefe stood there, his brilliant eyes stormy. He had changed out of his funeral attire into riding gear. "I tried to catch you at the house," he bit off, almost accusingly, 'but you were pretty quick to get away."

A flicker of temper, born of high emotion, flashed over her face. It had been *the* most dreadful day. "Let me stop you there, Keefe. I was one of the last to leave. Your grandmother didn't want me to stray too far from her side. I don't really know why." She broke off, her eyes filling with apprehension. "Is something the matter?" she asked quickly. "Surely not her?" Lady McGovern was eighty years old.

"No, no." Swiftly he reassured her. "She's retired, of course. Losing Dad has robbed her of all vigour. She was in fine form up until then. But God knows what will happen now! She's lost two sons. And a husband."

"I know," Skye said sadly. "In one way she has lived a life of privilege, but she has suffered a lot. Losing a child must be the greatest loss a woman can ever know." Her head was aching so much she ripped at the pins in her hair, pulling them out one by one and setting them down on the small table by the door. Afterwards she shook her hair free with a sigh of relief, letting it settle into shining masses around her face and shoulders.

"Sometimes you're so beautiful I can hardly endure looking at you," Keefe said abruptly. He reached out suddenly for a handful of her hair, twining it around his hand, pulling on it slightly to draw her closer to him.

"You haven't had to endure me of late," she reminded him with a flare of bitterness.

"Your decision." His tone was just as harsh. He released the silky swathe of her hair. "Can you do something for me, Skye?"

She relented. She had to on this day of days. "Of course I can." She could see the pressure that had been building in him all day. There was a faint pallor beneath his tan. Another sign of his anguish.

"Then get out of that dress." His tone was so short it sounded like an order. "I have the most desperate need to get away from the house. Put your riding gear on. Don't tell me you didn't bring it. I need to ride off some of this torment. It's all been such a nightmare. Dad gone. The memory of that last morning. So businesslike, so matter-of-fact. I never got a chance to tell him how much I loved him, admired and respected him. He was my role model."

"Keefe, he *knew*!" She wanted desperately to touch him but held herself back with an effort of will. "You're everything he wanted and needed in his son, his successor. He knew the empire he built was safe with you. He never mentioned your name without it ringing with love and pride."

He turned his dark head away, his skin drawn taut over his chiselled bones. "Do what I ask. I want to gallop until I drop."

"Why *me*?" She issued it like a challenge. "You have a brother, a sister, yet you come looking for me."

"Of course, *you*," he responded roughly. "Who else?"

It was mutual validation of sorts. "I don't understand you, Keefe," she said on a note of despair. "You push me away. You draw me back in. You make life a heaven and a hell."

"Maybe I only feel complete when you're around." He turned to her with intensity. "I missed you. You didn't come."

That almost sent her over the edge. "You surely didn't think I was about to forgive you for breaking my heart?" she cried fiercely. "You showered me with affection, Keefe. As a child, as an adolescent. You made sure I was never lonely. Your kindness and your patience. It's all etched into my memory. You might have been years and years older instead of only six. Then I grew up. And you took it all away. But not before you took *me*." Her blue eyes blazed.

Colour rose in a tide under his bronzed skin. "It was what *you* wanted." He grasped her by two arms, agony in his expression. "What *I* wanted. Neither of us could stop it. Neither of us tried. It was like it was ordained. Knowing your body meant everything in the world to me, Skye. Don't ever forget it, or downgrade it. It was another stage in our incredible bonding. The intimacy. I have a sister who's struggled all her life with jealousy of you. Consider her feelings for a moment. It was *you* I loved. *You*, Skye. You were so full of life and fun and endless intelligent questions. You *sparkled*. I love Rachelle. She's family. We share the same blood but, terrible to say, often times I don't *like* her."

"And you think you should?" Skye asked a little wildly. "Rachelle was never nice to me. Not for one single minute. She let her jealousy eat her up. Anyway, it's not unusual not to like someone in your family, though I didn't have one, except Dad. Thing is, we can't pick our families. We can't always like them."

"I guess." A muscle throbbed along his jaw. "I have to contend with Scott's jealousy as well. The two of them, my sister and my brother, ruining their lives with jealousy and re-sentment. Neither of them will find a life for themselves. Rachelle won't consider getting herself a job. There are things she could do, but she's falls back on her trust fund. Who knows what Scott's thought processes are? I've offered him Moorali Downs. It's a chance for him to find his feet. But no! It's all about focusing his weird enmity on me."

"Maybe if he falls in love?" Skye suggested, feeling his distress and frustration. "Finds the right girl? Marries her?"

Keefe laughed grimly. "Scott's fantasy is all about *you*."

That hit her like a blow "But surely he's forgotten me." Her expression revealed she was shocked and appalled. "I saw him with Jemma. She's a very nice young woman."

"Who is wasting her time." Keefe rejected that solution with a kind of anger. "I like Jemma too. She'll make some lucky man a fine wife but it won't be Scott. Scott's choice has to be *my* choice. Scott will always want the woman *I* want. As Gran once said, 'Scott wants to be *you,* Keefe'. That's his huge problem in life. Sibling rivalry is part of Scott's deepest being."

"Then that's a hell of a thing," she said. "Maybe he needs professional help."

"You think he doesn't realise it?" Keefe spoke with a mix of anger and sorrow. "Scott *does* have an insight into his own behaviour. He *knows* what drives him. The tragedy is he doesn't want to change things."

"So this is what it always comes to. I shouldn't have come back." Skye was painfully convinced it was so. "There's no place for me here, Keefe. I only make matters worse. Remember who I am."

His eyes flashed like summer lightning. "Who you are? I'll tell you. You're a beautiful, bright, accomplished woman. What more do you want? I don't give a damn that you were raised as Jack McCory's little motherless daughter. Jack is a good man. But who in God's name was your mother? That's the real question."

Her head shot up, all sorts of alarms going off. "What do you mean?"

"Why don't you have the courage to allow your concerns—our concerns—to leap to the centre?"

"I have no idea what you mean." She did. There were critical parts of her mother's life that were totally unknown.

"You do," he flatly contradicted, "but I can't handle it now. Take that black dress off, though heaven knows it makes your skin and your hair glow. Leave a note for Jack. Say you've gone riding with me. He'll understand."

"Of course he will!" She cut him off with something of his own clipped manner. "He's my father."

CHAPTER THREE

BIRDS shrieked, whistled, zoomed above their heads, filling the whole world with a wild symphony of sound. They had left the main compound far behind, driving the horses, initially unsettled and hard to saddle, at full gallop towards the line of sandhills, glowing like furnaces in the intermittent, blinding flashes of sun. Aboriginal chanting so ghostly it raised the short hairs on the nape at first floated with ease across the sacred landscape. Now the sound was fading as they thundered on their way.

From time to time crouching wallabies and kangaroos lifted their heads at their pounding progress, taking little time to get out of the way of the horses. Manes and tails flowing, they raced full pelt across the plains, their hooves churning up the pink parakeelya, the succulent the cattle fed on, and sending swirls of red dust into the baked air.

The heat of the day hadn't passed. It had become deadly. Thunderclouds formed thick blankets over a lowering sky. But as threatening as the sky looked—a city dweller would have been greatly worried they were in for an impending deluge—Skye, used to such displays, realised there might be little or no rain in those climbing masses of clouds. A painter would have inspiration for a stunning abstract using a palette of pearl grey, black, purple and silver with great washes of yellow and livid green.

Probably another false alarm, she thought, not that she cared if they got a good soaking. Any rain was a blessing. Her cotton shirt was plastered to her back. Sweat ran in rivulets between her breasts and down into her waistband. There could be lightning. There was a distant rumbling of thunder. She had seen terrifying lightning strikes. A neighbouring cattle baron had in fact been killed by a lightning strike not all that many years previously. Yet oddly she had no anxiety about anything. She was with Keefe.

Half an hour on, as if a staying hand had touched his shoulder, Keefe reined in his mount. Skye did the same. Riders and horses needed a rest. In a very short time the world had darkened, giving every appearance of a huge electrical storm sweeping in. It confirmed to her distressed mind this had been a very sad day. Wasn't that the message being carried across the vast reaches of the station by an elaborate network of sand drums? The chanting and the drums acted as powerful magic to see *Byamee,* Broderick McGovern, safely home to the spirit world.

Keefe took the lead, in desperate need of the quiet secrecy and sanctuary of the hill country. He loved and respected this whole ancient area, with all its implications. The ruined castles with their battlements had a strange mystique, an aloofness from the infinite, absolutely level plains country. It was as though they were secure in the knowledge it was *they* that had been there from the Dreamtime, created by the Great Beings on their walk-abouts. The hill country exerted a very real mystical force that had to be reckoned with. Many a Djinjara stockman, white or aboriginal, had over the years claimed they had experienced psychic terror in certain areas, a feeling of being watched when there was no other human being within miles. Keefe knew of many over time, including the incredibly brave explorers, who had tasted the same sensation around the great desert monuments that had stood for countless aeons, especially the Olgas, the aboriginal *Katajuta.* Ayer's Rock, *Uluru,* sacred to the desert tribes, was acknowledged as having a far more benign presence, whereas the extraordinary cupolas, minarets and domes of *Katajuta* projected a very different feeling.

They dismounted, their booted feet making deep footprints in the deep rust-red loam. They saw to the horses, then began moving as one up a sandstone slope to where stands of bauhinia, acacia, wilga and red mulga were offering shade. The powerful sun was sending out great sizzling golden rays that pierced the clouds and lit up the desert like some fantastic staged spectacle.

Skye knew this place well. She had been here many times, mostly with Keefe, at other times on her own to reflect and wonder. This was *Gungulla:* a favourable place. A place of permanent water and a camping spot for white man and aborigine alike. Up among the caves there were drinking holes in the form of big rock-enclosed bowls and basins. There was bush tucker too, all kinds of berries and buds packed with nutrition. One could survive here. She turned to witness a thrilling sight. The summits of the curling, twisting, billowing clouds were rimmed with orange fire.

Keefe had pulled a small blanket from his pack, letting it flap on the wind before spreading it on the sand beneath the clump of orchid trees. He looked up at Skye, standing poised above him, twirling a white bauhinia blossom with a crimson throat in her hand. She had picked the orchid-like flower off one of the trees as she had passed beneath. Keefe indicated that she should sit beside him. She did so, feeling a blend of longing and trepidation. Immediately the little sandhill devil lizards scurried for cover.

"I can't get my head around the fact my father is dead." Keefe spoke in an intense voice. "He was only in his mid-fifties. No great age these days. There's Gran eighty. Dad was *needed.*"

Sympathy and understanding were in her blue eyes. "His death has put a huge burden on you, Keefe. I know that. You thought you would have more years to grow into the job but the truth is you're ready. You can be at rest about that."

"Well, I'm not!" He wasn't bothering to conceal his grief from her. This was Skye. He was letting it out. "The numbers of us killed in light plane crashes!"

She couldn't argue with that. "But it can't prevent you from flying. Out here flying is a way of life. You were able to come for me."

He made a short bitter sound, more a rasp than a laugh. "I'd come for you no matter what."

She had to press her eyes shut. Block him out. "Don't fill my head with impossible dreams, Keefe." Goaded, she pitched the bauhinia blossom aside. He had hurt her so deeply the wounds would never heal. Yet here she was again defying all common sense.

"Do you dream of me?" he asked abruptly.

It took her breath.

"I dream of *you,*" he said, lying back on the rough grey blanket and staring up at the sky.

She looked down at his dark, brooding face. "If we weren't who we are, would you marry me?" How absurd could she get? She waited. He didn't speak so she answered her own question. "I think not." All these years wasted. Only they were unforgettable years. She would remember them to her last breath.

"Who *are* we exactly?" Abruptly he pulled her down to him in one swift, fluid motion.

She allowed him to do it even when she knew she could ill afford the least sign of surrender. To prove it, high emotion kicked in in a heartbeat. Keefe's sexual magnetism was unquestioned, and so proprietorial. He knew he owned her. That alone aroused a certain female hostility. Being *owned* was wrong.

"Are you saying there are secrets, Keefe?" She turned on her side to challenge him. They were so close, the pain was scarcely to be borne. Whatever had happened between them, they could never truly lose the old unifying bond. In his own way he needed her. But never as much as she needed him. There was nothing really normal about their relationship, she thought.

Again he didn't speak. Groaning with frustration, she flung her arm across his hard, muscled chest, feeling the rhythmic thud of his heart beneath her hand. Sometimes she thought she would simply expire with the pain of loving Keefe, when there seemed to be no resolution to the matter. It was here, almost this very spot, where he had first made love to her. Taken her virginity. Captured her heart. Held it so fast he had denied her the freedom to enjoy another lover for a long time. Even then, those few relationships had never taken real shape. There was no one like Keefe. The way he made love to her. The things he did. The things he said. It was magic and music. Unforgettable.

"Secrets, yes," he muttered. With a strong arm he fitted her body to him, as though her proximity gave him all the comfort this world could offer. "But does every secret need to be told?"

Her vulnerable flesh was pulsing with desire, causing deep knife-like sensations in her groin. He hadn't asked a rhetorical question. He needed an answer. "You're saying not every secret needs to be exposed to the light? Are you worried I'm *family,* Keefe?" Finally she threw her hidden anxieties into the ring.

"Isn't that the fear locked away in your own Pandora's box?" he countered, a correspondingly sharp note in his voice. "Let it out and who knows what will happen? Family!" he groaned. "There's nothing *family* about the way I feel about you."

Such an admission, yet she had a fierce desire to lash out at him. "*Feel,* certainly. Never *act* on those feelings. They could be taboo." Why not hurt him as he always managed to hurt her? "Just give me a simple answer. What *do* you feel?" She stared at him with her black-fringed radiant blue eyes.

He brushed the question aside as if she had wasted her breath asking it. "Is that some kind of a joke? Neither of us can let go of the other. More to the point, I need to ask, is it a safe time for you?" There was a great urgency in him she couldn't fail to miss.

"Safe?" She considered that with a brittle laugh. "No time is safe with you." She didn't think she could withstand the heat of his scrutiny. "Oh, Keefe!" Her breast rose and fell with her deep troubled sigh. Impossible to sustain the illusion she was her own woman. She was a woman who couldn't let go. Worse, he wouldn't *let* her go.

He shifted position, half pinning her beneath his powerful body but withholding most of his weight. "I want to make love to you. Tell me you'll let me?" The very first sight of her at the airport had triggered a desperate need in him for the mind-bending pleasure of knowing her body again. He needed her to lessen the pain of this dreadful chaotic day. Make it bearable.

"It's always what *you* want," she said. "Shades of the old *droit de seigneur!*" Tears sparkled in her eyes.

"Never heard of it," he darkly mocked, lifting skeins of her golden hair then letting them slide through his fingers. "I said, only if *you* want it."

"What a concession, Keefe!" Hostility was coming off her like steam. She knew it had its genesis in status. His. Hers. Though successive generations were easing up on the status war. Once it would have been considered a disgrace for the scion of a great pastoral family to become involved with the daughter of a lowly employee. But *she* was an educated woman living in the twenty-first century. She could take her place anywhere. Except, it seemed, at Djinjara.

"Do I want it?" She considered his question bleakly. With a tremendous effort of will she exerted enough strength to break free of him. High time she made it perfectly plain she was her own woman. "Do you really believe I'm happy to think of myself as a woman possessed?" A high flush of colour had come to her cheeks.

"Possessed and possessing," he answered bluntly. His hand, with a life of its own, moved up to caress her breast, shaping its contours within his palm, his thumb teasing the berry-ripe nipple. "I can feel your heart racing. It beats for *me*."

The truth of it cut her to the bone. One had an intellectual life. And one had an emotional life. Sometimes the two were at war. "So arrogant!" she lamented. "I exist only to worship at your feet?" Deliberately she removed his hand from her breast. She knew about love. She knew about total seduction. He had long since mastered the art.

"Maybe I am arrogant," he agreed flatly. "Maybe that's what you do to me, Skye."

He resumed his position, in all probability waiting for her to come round. Instead, she sat rigid with self-control, watching an eagle hawk swoop on its prey. "Are you ever going to free me, Keefe?" she asked eventually. "Or are you just holding onto me until you find someone else?"

He didn't appear to be listening to her. As though what she was saying made no sense to him. "This is almost the precise spot where I first made love to you," he said in a quiet, serious voice, an element of—was it regret?—in his tone.

"The heir to Djinjara having sex with the young daughter of a station employee."

Again he didn't choose to hear her. "The world was perfect that day. You made me feel like a titan. Capable of taking on the world. Sweet, funny little Skye with her ceaseless questions grown into a beautiful woman."

"You always took the time to answer those questions."

"They were always so intelligent. You had a great thirst for knowledge."

Her released breath had a soft, shaken sound. "You were

so kind to me in those days. Then overnight you drew back. You kept your distance. "

His handsome features tightened. "What would you have had me do? Keeping a distance between us was the only course open to me."

"Of course." There was brittle acceptance in her tone. "Keefe McGovern and Skye McCory. What a no-no! That was never going to work." Her gaze went beyond him. "It's going to storm."

He didn't move. "Right this minute I don't care if we're heading for Armageddon. I want to *crush* you. You won't let me. I want to take every little particle of you into me."

"That would seem to be our misfortune," she said with the greatest irony.

"I call it destiny." Abruptly he sat up. "I've missed you so much, Skye. You were supposed to come in August."

To be here with him, remote from everyone and everything, and hold herself aloof was an excruciating test of her resolve. "And sow more discord?" she challenged. 'No, Keefe, I couldn't. What was the point? Besides, you might have found yourself a fiancée by then."

His expression hardened. "Be damned to that! Haven't you forgotten something?"

"And what is that?" She spoke in a strung-out voice, knowing she was coming close to tumbling over the edge.

"*You're* the only woman I want."

The admission was like a blinding illumination.

Isn't that your lifetime passion? said the voice in her head. *To be Keefe's woman?*

When she spoke she spoke sadly. "The things you say are enough to blow my mind. *I'm* the only woman you want? If that's true—if I can possibly believe you—what in heaven or hell is wrong with us both?"

"Nothing good, it seems." On a wave of agitation he reached out to pull her back into his arms.

He was strong….so strong…the male scent of him the most powerful aphrodisiac. Pride made her put up a struggle of sorts, her blonde head lolling away from him, her eyes glistening with tears. Was there something missing in her that left her so vulnerable?

"Skye, please. Don't fight me," he begged.

"Can't you see I *must*?" She had to find it within herself to pull back from this point of no return.

"No, *don't*!" He lowered his head, hungrily covering her mouth with his own. His tongue lapped the moistness that slicked her full lips like it was the most luscious of wines. "Don't, don't, don't!"

Her heart contracted; her senses reeled. Desire came at her in an annihilating rush. This was black magic at its highest level. Keefe was the magician, ready to transport her to a different world. All she had to do was give herself up to his stunning sexual supremacy. His hands were moving down over her body. Soon she would stop thinking altogether. Mind and body would become two entirely separate regions.

Only…she couldn't shed all her painful memories like a snake shed its skin. Memories had the power to come crashing through. She wanted him desperately—she was *starving* for what only he could give her—yet she gathered herself sufficiently to pull away. Perhaps she should have pulled away that *first* time. Said *No, Keefe,* instead of *Yes, Keefe* and saved herself a whole world of pain. Memory opened up like a book…

Second-year exams were over. She thought she had done well. She had promised her closest girlfriend Kylie Mitchell— a fellow law student—she would spend part of the long summer vacation with her and her family at their beautiful beach hide-away on one of the Great Barrier Reef islands, but she was to spend Christmas and the New Year with her father. He was so looking forward to seeing her it was impossible to disappoint him, even if she knew she was going back into the lion's den. She hadn't forgotten Scott's near-assault on her. Mercifully it had never been repeated. In his heart Scott knew his brother would destroy him if he ever hurt her. From her sixteenth year, she had become off limits to Scott and his attentions. But from that day on she had never trusted him. On the surface they managed to get by quite well. There were pleasantries and jokes, but Skye thought she always saw at the back of Scott's eyes a familiarity bordering on insolence that exposed what was really at his heart.

Scott still fancied her. The only thing that stopped him from doing something about it was fear of swift retribution from his brother. From time to time Skye had rather horrible nightmares about Scott coming after her. Then, when it seemed he was about to physically overcome her, Keefe was always there to rescue her.

Keefe, her knight in shining armour. Only *confusion* reigned. Keefe remained her knight, but his whole attitude towards her had changed. It was as though she had lost her sweet innocence and turned into some sort of siren. In short, Keefe kept her at a distance. Just as he made sure his brother maintained a safe distance from her, he maintained that distance himself. What had happened that summer years ago had caused Keefe to shut a door on her.

A big Christmas Eve party was being held at the House. Lady McGovern herself had issued Skye an invitation.

"I won't take no for an answer, Skye,' she said, gauging from the expression on Skye's face she was about to make some excuse. "Your father won't mind in the least. You're a beautiful, clever young woman. A credit to us all. Quite a few young members of the family will be here. You'll enjoy yourself. Have you something pretty to wear?"

Luckily the perfect get-out had been handed to her on a

plate. "Nothing to wear to a party, Lady McGovern, I'm afraid. You must excuse me, but thank you so much for thinking of me. I know you'll understand I'd feel awkward and out of place in the one dress I've brought with me. It's a cotton sundress. I'm sure Rachelle and her cousins will be beautifully turned out."

"So they will," Lady McGovern agreed with an unsmiling nod. Rachelle's cousins, all from wealthy families, were out earning their own money, carving out careers, not relying on trust funds like Rachelle. Nothing she said made any difference to her granddaughter. Rachelle lacked drive. Worse, she had no sense of reality. Her feet didn't even touch the ground. That's what wealth did to some people. Why bother earning money when you had plenty? Here in front of her was young Skye McCory—the image of her mother—taking up life and developing her character. At the end of Skye's first year of law she was among the top five students. Lady McGovern fully expected she would repeat or even gain standing when the results for year two were posted in the New Year.

"Don't worry about that," she said, fixing Skye with her regal stare. "I took the opportunity of having something appropriate for you to wear sent in from Sydney. Think of it as an extra Christmas present." Djinjara's staff were given suitable Christmas presents. It was a long-standing tradition, as was their big New Year's Eve party held in the Great Hall. "Come along with me and I'll show it to you." The civility of the tone didn't conceal the fact it was an order. "Shoes to match so don't worry about them either. I have countless evening bags. I'm sure you can pick out something from among them."

Skye, at twenty, felt overwhelmed. "But Lady McGovern—"

"No buts about it!" The old lady turned on her, her tone so sharp it was like a rap over the knuckles. "Come along now."

Skye knew better than to argue.

* * *

As always, Rachelle was on hand to upset her.

She was almost at the front door when Rachelle tore down the grand staircase. "What have you got there?" she demanded, her dark eyes riveted to the long, elegant box in Skye's hands with its distinctive packaging and label.

Normally poised in the face of Rachelle's obvious dislike, Skye felt acute embarrassment. Colour swept hotly into her cheeks. "Lady McGovern has been kind enough to give me my Christmas present," she said.

"A dress?" Rachelle's upper-crust voice rose to a screech. "How come you rate a dress from Margaux's?" She advanced on Skye, looking shocked to her roots. Margaux's was arguably Sydney's top boutique, carrying designer labels from all over the world.

"Yes, a dress, Rachelle." Skye was recovering somewhat. "I'm thrilled."

"So you should be!" Rachelle's tone lashed. "Gran hasn't asked you to come to the Christmas Eve party surely?"

Skye held her temper. "She has. I'm sorry if that upsets you, Rachelle. I'll endeavour to keep out of your way."

Rachelle's face registered a whole range of emotions, fury uppermost. "I don't believe this!" she cried. "How could Gran do this to me?" Her eyes abruptly narrowed to slits. "I believe you begged her for an invitation. That's it, isn't it? You'd have the hide!"

"Wrong again." Skye shook her blonde head. "If you ask your grandmother, you'll learn the truth. But do remember to ask nicely. You're losing all your manners."

"I hate you, Skye McCory." As if she needed to, Rachelle laid it on the line. A McGovern to a McCory. A McGovern with a streak of vengeance.

"You have no right to," Skye replied, keeping her tone level, although she felt sick to her stomach. She was sick of

Rachelle's drama. In fact, she wanted to pitch the elegant box at this appalling young woman's head.

She had to walk away.

Right now.

The McGoverns still had her in their power, even if she was subsidising her own way with two part-time jobs. Beggars couldn't be choosers. But she had long since made the vow she would repay every last penny she owed them, even if it took years.

Surely her skin had never looked so luminous? Her thick, deeply waving honey-blonde hair formed a corona around her excited flushed face, animated to radiance. She couldn't help but be thrilled by the way she looked. She had never expected to own a dress like this. Not for years yet, and then she would have to be earning a darned good salary. It was gossamer light, the most beautiful shade of blue that, like magic, turned her eyes to blue-violet. The fabric was silk chiffon, with jewelled detailing, the bodice strapless, draped tightly around her body to the hips, from where it fell beautifully to just clear of her ankles. Her evening sandals—like the dress a perfect fit—were silver, as was her little evening bag that inside bore a famous Paris label.

"Oh, my darling girl, aren't *you* dolled up!" her father exclaimed in pride and pleasure when she presented herself for his inspection. "You look every inch a princess! I'm enormously proud of you, Skye. If only your mother was here to share this moment!"

Always Cathy, her mother. For her father there had never been any other woman. "I'm enormously proud of *you*, Dad," she countered, giving him a hug. "I suppose we'd better get going." Her father was to drive her up to the homestead, which was blazing with light.

"You enjoy yourself, hear me," her father urged as she

alighted from the station Jeep. "Don't let that Rachelle get under your skin. Poor girl has problems."

Skye, blessed with a generous heart, hoped Rachelle would one day solve them.

Days later she was still in a daydream, her head crammed with the long silent looks Keefe had given her that splendid Christmas Eve. All the other looks and stares. Many had looked for a very long time at Skye McCory in their midst, but the close attention had slid off her like water off a duck's back. What she hadn't realised was she had the arresting air of someone not conscious of her own beauty. Her looks were simply a part of her. Part of her genetic inheritance. She wasn't and never would be burdened by personal vanity. Rachelle of the patrician features was a beauty. But Rachelle brought to mind the old saying that beauty was only skin deep. Far better a beautiful nature. A beautiful nature could not be ravaged by time.

But the way *Keefe* had looked at her! It had made her feel rapturous, yet madly restless, like her body was a high-revving machine. Not like the old days when she had still been a child. Like a *woman*. A woman he desired. Her own feelings were still locked in the realms of dreams, but Keefe had looked at her as if *anything* were possible. He was the Prince who could claim his Cinderella. For Cinderella she was. At least to the McGoverns. That evening had been the most disturbing, the most exciting night of her life. She didn't think her memories would ever fade.

Had Keefe forgiven her for having distracted his brother? Lord knew, it hadn't been deliberate. Did he finally understand that? She had given Scott not the slightest encouragement. It was Scott who had had the willful drive to take what he wanted. With Keefe, it was like the start of something quite new and wondrously strange. A wonderful, sumptuous, brilliant night of tens of thousands of glittering stars and the Southern Cross hanging overDjinjara's huge tiled roof. Some memories lasted for ever.

She took her camera out to the sandhills. She had become very interested in photography since attending university. Her friend, Ewan, a fellow law student, had introduced a few of the others to the art form, fanning their enthusiasm to the point they had all pored over the various magazines on the market once they had moved past the basic techniques. The best magazines had taught her how to get great outdoor shots. She had quickly moved onto the intermediate level, such was her eye and her interest.

"You have an amazing talent, Skye!" Ewan had said, quite without envy. He had a big talent himself. "You're a born photographer. You should give up law."

"As though I could find work as a photographer!" she had scoffed. "If I'm so good, why don't you all chip in and buy me a decent camera?" Of course she had been joking but to her shocked delight Ewan had run around with the hat, raising close to eight hundred dollars with a very nice contribution from a top woman lecturer who admired Skye's work.

Skye had read up on all the great photographers, including Ansel Adams, recognised as one of the finest landscape photographers of all time. Landscape had been what she was particularly interested in. Considering where she had been born and lived, the savagely beautiful Channel Country, the home of the nation's cattle kings, was high up on her list of must-take photographs. She had thought she might even be able to make a bit of a name for herself, but she wasn't all that hopeful. Ewan, now, was far more interested in people. He had taken numerous photographs of her, which had captured her essence, according to her friends. The only time she had ever turned Ewan down had been when he had wanted to photo-

graph her nude. Not that the shots wouldn't have been tasteful.
Ewan was dead serious about his work. It was just that she was
too darned modest—modesty, had she known it, was part of
her charm—and she had been worried where the photographs
might eventually turn up. Ewan had already been offered a
showing at one of the small but interesting galleries.

That afternoon she had taken herself out to the hill country
with her brand-new camera. In a year she had raised enough
money on her own to trade in the camera her friends' gen-
erosity had bought her for the next model. The new camera
had many extras, options and problem-solving capabilities. It
had already augmented her natural ability to capture just the
image she was striving for. She was starting to think of herself
as a photographic artist seriously setting about taking impressions of her own country. On Djinjara there were countless special locations. Even then one needed patience for just
the right light, just the right shot. She intended to wait it out
to capture the amazing vibrance of an Outback sunset. City
people didn't realise the fantastic range and depth of colour
or the three-dimensional nature of the clouds. Outback sunsets
and sunrises were overwhelmingly beautiful. In them one
could see the hand of God.

Of special interest to her were the ghost gums. What wonderful trees they were, with their pure white silky-to-the-touch
boles. They made such a brilliant contrast to the rich red soil
and the bright violet-blue sky. She was lying on her back,
trying to get as low as possible so she could get in as much as
she could of the trees and their wonderful sculptural branches

That was the way Keefe found her. He must have spotted the
station Jeep at the base of the foothills and followed her trail.
He knew about her burgeoning interest in photography but he
hadn't as yet seen her work. She and Keefe were separated these
days, weren't they? But in their own way they remained tied.

It was really strange, the connection. A silver cord that could never be cut.

"Won't be a minute," she said, trying to bring full concentration back to her shot. She had been thinking so much about Keefe lately she had almost driven herself crazy.

"Take your time." With a faint sigh he lowered his lean frame onto a nearby boulder. Curiously it was shaped like a primitive chair, the back and the seat carved and smoothed to a high polish over aeons.

"I was hoping to take a few shots of the sunset," she explained, beginning to get up. "Djinjara's sunsets are glorious."

He stood immediately, put out a hand, helped her to her feet.

Skin on skin. For a disconcerting moment it was almost as though he had pressed her hand to his lips. How susceptible was the flesh! It had been a blazingly hot day so she was wearing brief denim shorts and a pink cotton shirt tied loosely at the waist over one of her bikini tops. Quite a bit of her was on show. She wasn't supposed to be on show, was she?

"You're really into this, aren't you?" he asked, a trace of the old indulgence in his voice.

"Love it," she said, whisking a long shining wave of her hair off her flushed face. She had tied it back in a ponytail but the wind had gone to work on the neat arrangement. "It would take a lifetime but one of my ambitions is to photograph as much as I can of our great untouched land," she confided, knowing he would understand. No one loved the land more than Keefe. The land was a passion they shared. "I can't wait for the miracle of the wildflowers."

"Your special time," he said.

His diamond-bright eyes moved to rest on her with such an unsettlingly tender expression that her body might have been a long-stemmed blossom.

"*Our* special time." She managed a smile, tingling to the tips of her fingers. "I loved every moment I spent with you as a child. But those were the halcyon days, weren't they? We've moved on."

"*You've* moved on," he said, a touch grimly. "*I'm* still here."

"You wouldn't be anywhere else," she scoffed.

"Don't you miss it?" He leaned into the boulder with a characteristically elegant slouch. Keefe had such grace of movement. He had discarded his wide-brimmed hat, his luxuriant black hair thick and tousled, his darkly tanned skin glittering with the lightest sweat.

"Of course I miss it!" she said fervently, betraying her sense of loss. "I'll probably miss it all my life."

"So what's your life going to be, Skye?" he questioned, his eyes a sharply observant silver.

"I haven't figured that out yet." Immediately she was on the defensive.

"Well, you're only twenty." He shrugged. "But you must have a whole string of admirers by now?"

"No more than you," she shot back.

"Now you're being ridiculous."

"I'm not being ridiculous at all," she said heatedly. "What about Fiona Fraser? She stayed glued to your side at the party. Then there's Clementine. I like Clemmie. Your second cousin Angela has become very glamorous. And she's a gifted pianist."

"So she is," he nodded. "A conservatorium graduate. Angela is a city girl."

"Here we go!" she answered breezily. "That counts *her* out, then. City girls are trouble. So we're back to Fiona."

"*You're* back to Fiona, and I thought you were a hell of a lot smarter. I'm twenty-six years old, Skye. Twenty-six to your twenty. I have no thought of marriage on my mind."

"As yet. You have to be aware you're one of the biggest catches in the country.' It came to her that she was deliberately winding him up. It was really crazy of her, wanting to pick a fight.

"Then you know way more than I do." He dismissed that impatiently. "I'm the guy who's being groomed to one day take over not only a cattle empire but Dad's numerous business interests as well. We've been diversifying for a long time now."

"No one ever said the McGoverns weren't smart." She made a wry face, one hand making a move to button up her shirt. Only it was too darned obvious. The bikini top was pretty skimpy. Not that Keefe was looking at her in *that* way. The sad thing was he could arouse her most potent, erotic feelings with a single glance.

She wanted…wanted… What *did* she want? She was still a virgin. No frustration attached to that state. She had plenty of friends. Male and female. It was simply that no young man she had met had come close to measuring up to Keefe. That was the pity of it.

A pity beyond all telling is hid in the heart of love. Blake, his "Songs of Innocence". She felt like an innocent, a babe in the woods.

There was a frown on Keefe's dynamic face as he watched her. "Don't you feel safe here, Skye?" he asked.

The seriousness of his tone cut across her reverie. "What a question!" Her hand dropped to her side. Why was she so nervous of revealing her body to Keefe? She was oblivious to all the stares she received whenever she visited a beach. Then she thought: *It's Keefe! It's always Keefe.*

Dusk was closing in. Shrieking, the legions of birds were starting to home into the density of trees that lined the maze of watercourses, lagoons, swamps and creeks on the station. It was an awe-inspiring sight, the sheer numbers.

"Answer it," Keefe said in a firm voice.

She stared at him. "You sound stressed."

"Maybe I am." He swatted at a dragonfly with iridescent wings. It seemed bent on landing on his head. "Scott won't bother you," he said, his expression formidable.

Scott? Scott wasn't even an afterthought. "I'm not worried about Scott, Keefe," she assured him quickly. "We're getting along. You warned him off. He heeded your message. You love your brother, don't you?"

He plunged an impatient hand through his hair, fingers splaying into the distinctive McGovern widow's peak. "Of course I do," he said edgily. "But like you I know he has a callous streak. I don't want to see that turned on women."

"Of course not!" She couldn't control a shudder, acutely aware he was monitoring her every movement and expression. "Is he interested in Jemma Templeton?" She knew for a fact Jemma had always had a crush on Scott.

"Why do you want to know?" His silver eyes blazed.

She swallowed at his tone. It was so clipped it provoked a flash of anger. "No particular reason," she answered shortly. "Just making conversation. *I* have no interest in Scott, Keefe. Take my word for it. "

It's you I love.

"Sometimes I get so tired of it all." Unexpectedly he made the admission. "Not the job. I can handle that. Handle the lot." He paused, studying her closely. "Nothing is the same between us, is it, Skye? The ease has gone with the wind."

He hadn't moved, yet she felt she had been taken into a passionate embrace. "You sound like you're grieving for what we lost." Despite that and the angst of his tone, she had an escalating sense of excitement, so intense she knew it was carrying her close to peril.

His silver eyes blazed. "If I touch you I'll make love to you. Do you *know* that?"

He had said it yet she seemed hardly able to take it in. Even her heart rocked in shock.

"No answer?"

She began to shiver in the dry heat. How *could* she answer? She needed time to react to the pulverising shock. Besides, his tone seemed as much savage as sensual, as though he had found himself unwillingly caught in a dilemma.

"Here in the shadow of the sand dunes with all the Dreamtime gods around us," he intoned. "I'm convinced this is a sacred place. That's one reason why I'd like to spread a blanket on the sand, take you down on it. You've always been little Skye to me. Now you've become pure desire." He spoke with such intensity his luminous eyes had darkened to slate grey. "I didn't tell you how beautiful you looked in your blue dress the other night."

Her stomach was churning, her limbs seized by trembling. Yet incredibly she said, "Maybe your eyes told me." Even her body was swaying towards him like a flower swayed towards the sun.

"Eventually I was bound to give myself away," he said, a twist to this mouth. "I'm sure I'll remember how you looked that night to the end of my days. No one wears the colour blue like you do."

Whatever he *said*, he wore the demeanour of a man who was in the process of making a hard decision. A decision he meant to stick by come what may. "I don't want to leave you here." He turned his head abruptly, his tone a shield. "It's getting late. You can come back tomorrow if you like. There's always another sunset."

"It's okay, I'll stay." He was hurting her, punishing her. For what? Growing up? Turning into a desirable woman? She could see the pulse drumming away in his temple.

"It's *me*, isn't it, Keefe?" She took a hesitant step towards him, her blue eyes full of entreaty. "*I'm* the one causing you tension. You don't really want me here. I've turned from your 'little buddy' into a woman, thus an unwanted distraction."

The air between them fairly crackled. "You want me to tell you that?" he challenged roughly. "Well, I *can't*. I do want you here, but my job is to *protect* you. It's always been my job. Gran really suffered when your mother died. Did you know that?"

Skye shook her head helplessly. Why was he going off at a tangent? And now? "No, I didn't," she admitted. "If she suffered, she must have loved my mother?"

"*Love*." He reached for her in a blind rush, hauling her right into his arms.

His grip was so powerful, so *perfect,* she felt as weightless as a china doll.

Breathe, Skye. Breathe. Her emotions were running so high, her response so headlong, it was possible she could pass out.

"*God!*" he breathed, turning up his head to the cobalt dome of the sky. It sounded to her ears like a cry for help. Like he knew he shouldn't do this. Whatever the desire he felt for her—she couldn't help but be aware of his arousal—he felt compelled not to give in to it. "We have to go. Really, we have to go." His grip eased abruptly so she could move.

Only she couldn't. She wanted to stay there with him for the rest of her life. Even if it sounded as if his heart was being torn out of him. That gave her wild hope. "No, stay here with me," she begged. Where had that alluring tone of voice come from? She had never used it before.

From the heart.

Unable to control the mad urge that had come upon her, she brought up her arms to lock them around his neck. The thought of having power over him was absolutely dizzying. She heard him groan like a man ensnared in some inescapable golden net. "What are you *doing* to me, Skye?" he muttered. "You *know* what will happen?"

"So?" Her eyes were devouring each separate feature of his face. The set of his extraordinary eyes. The arch of his black brows that formed such a stunning contrast. His tanned skin bore a prickle of dark beard. And, oh, his *mouth*! That wide, strong, sensual mouth, the outline so cleanly cut it might have been chiselled.

"You're a virgin?" He looked down into her eyes, his hands spreading out over her back burning through the cotton.

"I am." Her voice was scarcely above a whisper.

"You wouldn't lie to me."

It was a statement, not a question. Was he that sure of her? So aware she had an emotional dependency on him? "Are *you* lying in some way to me now, Keefe? Tormenting me? Or are you promising to take me where you believe I want to go?"

His handsome face showed stress. "Let me try."

All nature seemed to be listening. Even the birds, though they wheeled overhead, gave no cries to stay her. She should be listening too. Not making it so easy for Keefe to win her over. *"You?"* she questioned. "The never-puts-a-foot-wrong Keefe McGovern to cut loose with Jack McCory's daughter?"

"The more I try, the fiercer the longing gets." Keefe's answer was harsher than he had intended but he felt himself on a knife edge. Attraction this strong, this elemental rendered a man nearly powerless. Slowly he closed his roughened hands around the satin-smooth planes of her face, caressing her cheekbones as he would caress an exquisite piece of porcelain.

It was too much for Skye. Little silver sparks were dancing wildly in her breast. She had to close her eyes to contain the powerful shooting sensations. Excitement that had started as a dull roar was turning into a raging flame. If there was a taboo, it was about to be broken…

In the next breath she felt his mouth, warm and lushly *male,* come down over hers. He tasted wonderful! Delectable! She could scarcely get enough of him. Her knees were buckling from the sheer weight of emotion. She had to cling to him, throw her arms around his waist to anchor her to the ground. Sexual desire—no it was much more: an undying *passion*—was mounting at such a rate it had become a turbulent flood of hunger ready to surge over her and take her under. Keefe did things better than anyone. Better than anyone *could.*

Keefe drew her lips up with his own, taking deeply erotic exploratory breaths, sipping and sucking at the sweet nectar within, while he continued to hold her against him with un-knowing strength. The intimacy was so intense it was almost unbearable. The light clear pure bonds of childhood had turned into an adult force so powerful it was intimidating. He had always looked at her with such fondness, like a much-loved little cousin, with respect for her high intelligence. How, then, could he allow himself to become a threat to her? Worse, possibly destroy what they had?

"Is it wrong to go from protector to lover?" he asked, never more serious in his life. He drew back quickly so he could search her face. He couldn't believe how beautiful she looked, or how highly aroused. Her beauty and desirability leapt at him.

He had to bend low to hear her whispered answer. "Couldn't we see it as entirely natural?" she asked. He was so absolutely perfect to her in every way. No one could replace him.

"Then God will forgive me," Keefe answered in a strange near-mystical tone. What had befallen him had befallen her.

Kismet.

Skye allowed her heavy lids to fall shut. She felt as though Heaven had given her permission to allow ascendancy to the blind yearning she felt. This moment in time had been accorded her. Therefore she had to seize on it, feeling like a mortal maiden about to couple with a young god.

CHAPTER FOUR

The Present

HER father sat down to a dinner with a sad and haunted look in his eyes. The colour was a bright blue like hers but they were a different shape.

"I'm glad you went riding with Keefe," he said, picking up his knife and fork. "He mightn't have shown it but he was really labouring to get through today."

"I know, Dad." For a moment she wondered if denying Keefe the comfort of her body was not a failure on her part. For his part, he had accepted her decision and moved on.

"This looks great, love!" Jack praised the unfamiliar dish.

Skye had to smile. He was her dad. He was forever praising her. Everything she did was just great.

"Thai stir-fried beef with a few vegetables and noodles. Hope you like it."

"I like anything you make," he told her, quite unnecessarily. "How did you turn into such a good cook?"

"I took lessons in the city," she said, forking a slice of bell pepper. "Everyone should be able to cook. I enjoy cooking. I'm quite domesticated, really."

"You know what? So was your mother!" The sad expression lifted like magic. "Cathy was a bonzer little cook. Very fancy. Presented a meal beautifully. Not like your poor old dad. It's steak and chips mostly and lashings of tomato sauce. At least the steak is prime Djinjara beef. Tender enough to melt in your mouth." Jack paused, to look directly into his daughter's eyes. "I thought I spotted a bit of tension between you and Keefe when you arrived. I was pretty keyed up myself."

"Why wouldn't you be?" she replied gravely. "Mr McGovern's death came as a terrible shock. As for Keefe and me, nothing is as easy as the old days, Dad. They're gone. We're adults now. I have to accept it. Keefe is Keefe, Master of Djinjara and everything else besides. It's a huge job he's taken on. In many ways it's been unfair. There's always been great pressure on Keefe. Little or no pressure on Scott. All Rachelle has to do is marry more money."

"She won't be an easy target," Jack pronounced. "Keefe will have been left in charge of the McGovern Trust. No fortune-hunter will get past him."

"Well, I don't wish any bad experience on Rachelle," Skye said. "You'd think she'd interest herself in one or other of the McGovern enterprises. I'm sure she'd make a good business-woman if she tried."

Jack looked unconvinced. "Very unpleasant young woman, I'm sorry to say." Jack was never the one to talk badly of anyone. "No one likes her. She's an outstanding example of a first-class snob, when Keefe, the heir, is anything but. Don't worry about Keefe, love. I know what he means to you. He's up to the job. Count on it. I've never seen a man prouder of his son than Mr McGovern was of Keefe."

"True, but he had *two* sons, Dad," Skye felt obliged to point out. "Perhaps without meaning to Mr McGovern, while lavishing his love and pride on Keefe, turned Scott into a bitter young man." She pondered that a moment, then rejected it. Broderick McGovern had loved both his sons.

"No, dear." Jack McCory shook his head. "Scott sprang from his poor mother's womb, bitter."

"Seems like it!" Skye gave a regretful sigh. "Still, many gifts and attributes were showered on Keefe at birth. Not the other son."

"Not simply the luck of the draw, Skye. Mr McGovern did love Scott. He worried about Scott's mood changes. Scott was given every opportunity to make a success of himself with that job on Moorali. It would have been a big leg up. He turned it down flat. Both Scott and Rachelle take after the mother's family, the Crowthers. Mrs McGovern was never really at home on Djinjara, although as a Crowther she was Outback born and raised. Rachelle is like her, in looks as well."

"I barely remember her," Skye said. "Lady McGovern has always ruled. I must have been ten or eleven when Keefe's mother died. Melanoma wasn't it?"

Jack nodded.

Skye set down her knife and fork seeing an opening. "We never talk about *my* mother, Dad. There's only one *good* photograph of her in the house."

"And aren't you the image of her!" Jack exclaimed. "Even then I couldn't take it out for years and years. The pain of loss was too great. That's the danger in giving your heart away."

Gently she touched his hand. "Dad, I understand the pain—"

"No, darlin', you *don't*," Jack said with conviction. "You only *think* you know. One has to experience the death of that beloved person to know the total devastation. I wouldn't wish it on anyone."

"Of course not." Skye felt chastened, but determined to persevere. "Lady McGovern avoids the whole subject, as you do. It's like venturing into dangerous territory, but you must understand, Dad, there are things I want to know, things it's taken me far too long to ask." Like who *exactly* was my mother? That was the issue Keefe had referred to as a "Pandora's box".

Jack's head shot up. "Oh, darling girl, I'm sorry. I'm just plain selfish," he apologised. "All I've thought of is my own pain, my own loss. You'll have to forgive me. The worst of the pain—the most brutal, heart-wrenching grief—has eased. A man couldn't continue to live with it. But I can never forget. I loved my Cathy with all my heart. She died giving me the best and most beautiful daughter in the whole wide world."

Skye's eyes filled with tears. She rose from her chair to put her arms around her father's shoulders, kissing his weathered cheek. "All right, Dad, we won't talk now. Finish your meal. There's coconut ice cream with lime and ginger syrup for later. Maybe when we have our coffee you'll feel able to answer just a few of my questions."

Jack had his work cut out, giving his daughter a smile. When all was said and done there was a great deal about his beautiful Cathy *he* didn't know. Cathy had been such a private person not even he had been able to intrude.

Skye returned to her chair feeling a prickling of unease. If her mother had been a member of Lady McGovern's family in England—maybe extended family—what relationship did she herself bear to the McGovern family? According to legend, her mother was the daughter or niece of a friend of Lady McGovern's. No one knew exactly, it was all terribly vague. Deliberately vague. But why?

She was soon to discover her father knew amazingly little about his beautiful young wife's background….

"I married Cathy because I loved her, not because of any background," he said, resting back in his armchair. "She was like an angel from Heaven, bringing glory into my life. I couldn't *believe* it when she consented to marry me."

Skye had no difficulty accepting that. Wasn't her own situation with Keefe a reversal of the situation that had existed between her father and mother; the social divide which would have been far greater in their day? Then there was the issue regarding her mother's exact connection to the McGoverns. "But how did the relationship grow, Dad?" she asked, covering her bewilderment. "You were a stockman at the time. She was a guest of Lady McGovern. How could it be? Where did you meet? How often? How long did it take you to fall in love?" She knew from her father's expression that the whole topic was causing him distress, but she felt driven to continue.

"Me?" Jack's eyebrows shot up. "Why, the instant I laid eyes on her! And she *knew*. I must have given myself away that very day. She was so beautiful, so fresh and sweet. Nothing stuck-up about her. She was someone who spoke to everyone on the station. Everyone loved her. That love has been passed on to you. When I was out of it with grief, there was always someone keeping an eye on you. Lady McGovern placed you in Lena's care."

"And wonderful she was to me too!" Skye was still in contact with Lena, who now lived with a family in Alice Springs.

Jack nodded. "True blue was Lena. I tried once to get her to talk—fill me in about Cathy and her connection to the family—but Lena wouldn't open up. Still, I think Lena knew a lot."

"About what, specifically?" Maybe she could get more information out of Lena than her father if she tried?

"Oh, an amazing amount of stuff," Jack said, looking like he wanted to terminate the whole conversation. "I guess we should have had this discussion years ago, but in all truth, love, I never did know a lot. Cathy wouldn't talk about her past. She'd started a new life. With me. Whatever she wanted I went along with. So in a way I'm accountable for her death."

"No, Dad, *no!*" Skye protested strongly. "You have to stop all that. It was a tragedy."

"Yes, a tragedy," Jack groaned. "She died in my arms. My little Cathy. Do you suppose it could have been because you arrived early?"

This was way beyond Skye. There had never been any mention that she had been a premature baby. All her life she had enjoyed excellent health. Unease struck harder.

"Who attended the birth? Who was the doctor, the midwife, whatever?"

Jack's face was showing strain. "Tom Morris. A good bloke, a good doctor. He's dead now, Tom."

"Who called him?"

Jack looked stunned. "Why, Lady McGovern got him here fast. He was flown in. I remember him saying practically right off he had concerns."

"Why didn't she go to hospital?"

"She didn't *want* to," Jack said broken-heartedly. "She was adamant about it. She was happy to be on Djinjara. She loved it here. She loved being with me. *'You're my minder, Jack,'* she used to say with a laugh. I minded her. Yes, I did. Until the end. I don't know what her reasons were for leaving her own people. All I know is she found sanctuary with Lady McGovern. Lady McGovern used to talk to Cathy like she was her own child. Of course she wasn't. But I wouldn't be surprised to hear there was some blood connection."

"You don't know?"

"No, I don't, love." Jack shook his head. "And I wouldn't dare ask the old lady."

So her father had lived with his own demons. High time for her to face up to her own. Lady McGovern would know the truth. Probably she was the only one living who did. But she had the dismal notion Lady McGovern wasn't about to help anyone out. Bizarre as it sounded, even Broderick

McGovern might never have known a great deal about Cathy. He would have been married by then with a wife and children.

Time to visit her mother's grave. Then time to go back to her city life. Back to the life she had forged for herself. She had to confront the fact the same aura of unease regarding her background surrounded Keefe as it did her. Maybe the crucial bits that were missing explained why neither of them seemed able to move forward. Only Lady McGovern knew exactly what had happened all those years ago...

She took one of the horses to the McGovern graveyard, tethering the mare in the shade of the massive desert oaks. A huge wrought-iron fence enclosed the whole area, the iron railings topped by spikes. The gates were closed, but unlocked. She opened one side and walked through, shutting it with a soft clang behind her. This was the McGovern graveyard, scrupulously tended, with generations of McGoverns buried here. Everywhere there were markers and plaques, tall urns, a few statues. A classical-style white marble statue of a weeping maiden marked the grave of the wife of the McGovern founding father.

What was her mother doing, lying here among the McGoverns? She had asked Lady McGovern once when she had been about twelve and had failed to get any answer whatever. Just a stern silence. She had never asked again. Broderick McGovern's grave as yet had no headstone. No one had expected him to die so prematurely, leaving his son at barely thirty to take up the reins.

She had brought flowers with her. Not from the home gardens, though she could have asked and been given as many armfuls as she wanted. Instead, she had broken off several branches of pink and white bauhinia, arranging them in a sheaf. Oddly, although the cemetery wasn't a cheerful place, it wasn't depressing either. Surrounded by such incredible empty *vastness*, in the distance the ancient temples of the sandhills glowing an orange-red flame, it wasn't difficult to get one's own life into perspective.

Her mother's grave was marked by a child-sized white marble angel with outspread wings. The inscription read:

Catherine Margaret McCory, 1964-1986.
Do not stand at my grave and weep
I am not there

Silently she mouthed several more lines of the famous bereavement poem. She knew them by heart. All around her the silence was absolute except for the soft tranquil swish of the desert breeze. For an instant she fancied the breeze very sweetly kissed her cheek. Perhaps it was a greeting from her mother? Why not? It was hard to believe one simply ceased. There was mind, spirit. Only the body was consigned to the ground.

Cathy could well be in the thousand winds that blew, the swift uplifting rush of birds, the soft stars that shone at night. Though the stars that shone in their billions over Djinjara were ten times more brilliant than city-soft.

"Where are you, Cathy?" Without being aware of it Skye spoke aloud. "*Who* are you?" She desperately needed reassurances. Tears for what might have been pooled in her eyes. She bent to place the bauhinia branches, weighed down by exquisite blossom, on the white stone. There were so many mysteries in life. She couldn't seem to get to the bottom of the mystery of her own family. Had her mother lived she could have bombarded her with questions and got answers. She had always been a questioning child. Now it seemed her mother's short life had been defined by her death.

She paid her respects at Broderick McGovern's resting place then made her way slowly along the gravelled path to the tall gates. Along the way she passed a brilliant bank of honeysuckle that adorned one side of the fence, pausing to draw in the haunting perfume. Life might be many things, she thought, but in the end it all came down to one thing. Great or small, the body returned to dust. She chose to believe the soul roamed freely…

Just as she reached the gate, a station Jeep pulled up so hard it raised a great swirl of red dust and fallen dry leaves. Deliberate, Skye thought. Rachelle was at the wheel. Resolutely Skye turned to face her. She could hardly remount and gallop away. Unpleasant and abrupt as Rachelle was, this was Djinjara. Rachelle was a McGovern. She had to be accorded respect.

Rachelle was out of the vehicle with the speed of a rocket being fired. She was dressed in a cream silk shirt and jodhpurs, riding boots on her feet when it was well known Rachelle didn't particularly enjoy riding, though she was competent, as expected of a McGovern.

"What are you doing here?" Rachelle whipped off her big black designer sunglasses.

"I wonder you ask, Rachelle," Skye managed a quiet answer. "My mother is buried here."

"Highly unusual, I'd say." There were shadows under Rachelle's fine dark eyes. She looked faintly ill and nerveridden. Yet even in the tranquillity of the graveyard, with her father laid to rest not far away, Rachelle couldn't rein in her dislike and resentment.

"You should speak to your grandmother some time," Skye suggested. "She was very fond of my mother. My mother could only have been buried here with her approval."

"It's all seriously odd," Rachelle said, a vein throbbing in her temple. "That's all I can say. Your mother should be all but forgotten. *You* didn't know her. We were only little kids when she died yet we can't seem to get rid of her. Or *you* either."

Skye gave the other woman a saddened look. "Why do you hate me so much, Rachelle?"

Rachelle looked back with huge disbelief. "You don't know?" she hooted. "You robbed me of my brother for years and years of my life."

"No."

"You *did.*"

"Maybe he saw *you* weren't going to be my friend?"

"*Please!* You could never be numbered among my friends."

"Where *are* all your friends, Rachelle?" Skye retorted, suddenly firing up. "You didn't have any at school. I'm fairly modest by nature but you might recall *I* did. I was also head girl in my final year."

"How impressive!" Rachelle sneered. "Who knows why Gran wanted you there in the first place. I guess she had to be fond of your mother. Who was she anyway? Over twenty years have gone by and Gran won't say a word about her."

Wasn't that the truth! "You surely must know if she was a relative? One of Lady McGovern's relatives in England?" Skye challenged, so desperate for clues she would ask even Rachelle.

Rachelle's outraged expression rejected that. "I'd have a heart attack if I thought you and I were related," she snapped off. "Your mother was just some stray Gran befriended. I don't know from where. Like I care!"

"But you *do* care."

It had got to the stage where they all cared. "Nonsense!" Rachelle's cry was a near shriek. "You're the bane of my life, Skye McCory."

"Sounds like you should get a life," Skye advised, turning away.

"Keefe might have loved you when we were kids," Rachelle called after her. "But he doesn't love you now. *You'll* never get him. That's what he told me, I swear. Though I expect that cuts your heart to ribbons. You love him. Don't think I'm a fool. You've always loved him. But nothing will ever happen between you and him. Keefe has his life planned differently. He's way out of your league."

Skye had to wait until the initial shock had worn off. "Where did you learn to be such a terrible snob, Rachelle?" she asked quietly enough, though Rachelle's words had landed like punches.

"It's called knowing who you *are*," Rachelle explained with a lofty tilt of her chin. "I'm a McGovern. You're Jack McCory our overseer's kid. He's a real rough diamond, isn't he, your dad?"

Skye felt heat burn up her veins. *Steady. Steady.* She got herself under control. "He could teach *you* some manners," she answered with cool disdain. "I can see there's never going to be a way for us to start over, Rachelle. In a way, I'm sorry about that. I know you're not good at taking advice, but if I were you I'd jettison the bitterness and save your sanity. Hatred and jealousy hold bad karma."

"Bad karma?" Rachelle's laugh held more than a hint of ferocity. "Tell me about it! And what's this with Rob? He only stayed over thinking he could hang around you. Except Keefe put a sock in it and set him to work. Using Rob as a back-up, are you, dear? Can't have Keefe. Scott isn't interested. Maybe Robbie will do?"

Introducing Cousin Robert at this point caught Skye by surprise. She hadn't laid eyes on Rob since the day of the funeral.

"Well?" Rachelle gave Skye a disgusted look.

"Sorry, I need time to digest that, Rachelle. Rob is nice. I like him. But I have no romantic interest in him whatever."

"Maybe not but you do need a leg up in the world. A Sullivan would certainly do. But there again too much of a reach." Rachelle laughed with bitter triumph. "You're nothing but—"

She broke off hastily as a tall shadow fell. Both young women turned round to see Keefe standing barely a few feet away. How had he moved so silently? Skye marvelled. It didn't seem possible. But, then, Keefe managed to do some pretty incredible things.

"Is this really the place to have an argument?" he asked tersely, his light eyes blazing from one young woman to the other.

"Not an argument, Keefe." Colour flooded Rachelle's pale face. "I was laughing."

Keefe's expression would have daunted anyone. "If that was a laugh, Rachelle, you'd never get me to join in. Why are you always attacking Skye? Is it ever going to end? Skye has no interest in Rob. It's Rob who is out of his depth."

"Please, Keefe! Don't go on," Skye implored, seeing all Rachelle's bravado drain out like her life's blood. "Rachelle is very stressed. We all are. I came to pay my respects to your father and visit my mother's grave. I'll go now."

"Believe me, that's for the best," said Rachelle hoarsely, no more able to control herself than a two-year-old. "This is family. This is the family cemetery. I have fresh flowers in the Jeep for Dad. Are you going to join me, Keefe?" She swung her dark head to appeal to her brother.

"Yes," he returned sombrely, speaking directly to Skye. "No matter what happens, life goes on. We need to round up the best of the brumbies in the morning. We badly need a few more working horses. I thought you'd like to come along."

Rachelle moved closer to her brother. "Count me in. I'd like to come."

"I thought you regarded herding brumbies as a bad idea?" Keefe countered, looking down at his sister.

"Maybe I want to rediscover the thrill."

"Then I have to warn you, you might be sore and sorry the next day."

"What about *her*?" Rachelle countered, wearing a huge frown.

"Even you will have to admit Skye's a far better rider than you, Rachelle," Keefe said, keeping his tone level. "Also she keeps up with her riding when she's back in the city. I can't think when you last went out for a gallop, even if you do like to wear riding clothes. But I will say they suit you."

"I can keep up," Rachelle maintained stoutly. "I'll take one of the horses out this very afternoon. Give it a workout."

Keefe didn't answer, but turned back to Skye. "I'd like to make a pre-dawn start. Okay with you?"

The least contact with Rachelle left Skye feeling frayed. "Keefe, I think I'll pass," she told him quietly.

"You amaze me!" There was a satiric inflection in his voice. "Besides, you *can't* pass. I've counted you in."

They saddled up when Minghala, the dawn star, hung high in the east. It was still dark and the air was a good ten degrees cooler than it would be in only a few hours' time.

Keefe, sitting tall in the saddle, looked across to Skye. "Stick with me," he said.

"You got it, boss!" she mocked, touching a finger to the brim of her Akubra.

"You don't want to?" There was a twist to his mouth.

"It used to be much the best place to be." Their relationship was highly sexual but the strong attachment was also non-sexual. Their liking for each other, the interests they shared, their love of the land. It would always hold them together.

"Don't talk like it's history," he said.

And an odd history it was too! Swiftly she changed the subject. "I see you've allowed Rob to come along?' She looked towards the group of other riders. Rob Sullivan was a fine horseman and an excellent polo player. He often played on Keefe's team.

"Actually, Rob *begged* to come along," Keefe stressed. "He'll be an asset. I don't know about Rachelle." Rachelle made up the rest of the party along with three of the station's top aboriginal stockmen. All three had great tracking eyes— tracking was essential, demanding considerable skill—and a wonderful way with horses. One of them, Jonah, was ma- noeuvring his gelding back and forth in a parody of herding cattle. Everyone was mounted, circling the forecourt, getting the frisky horses under control.

"So where are we heading?" Skye could feel the build-up of excitement.

Keefe rode alongside her. "The mob has been spotted drinking near Jinjin Swamp. They could have moved on but some of the mares are carrying foals. That will slow them down."

"So who's the kingpin these days?" she asked, watching a very impatient-looking Rachelle scolding the horse she was riding. The mare *was* acting up a little, but there was no doubt Rachelle's bad mood was communicating itself to the animal.

"Still Old Man Mooki," Keefe said, lifting an arm and ges- turing to the north-west to mark their start. "He's still capable of impregnating the mares and he's still full of fight. Mooki is as wily as they come. He's no use to us, of course, but there are ten or twelve decent-looking colts running with him. We're after them."

"How many in the mob?" She looked towards the horizon, now washed with ever-expanding bands of pearl grey, pink and lemon.

"Around thirty last time we checked. I know you're good at this, but don't take any chances."

She responded to the seriousness of his tone. "I won't."

"You might keep an eye on Rachelle from time to time. I've asked Rob to do the same. He's got one hell of a crush on you, by the way, and not hiding it very well."

"Some men wear their hearts on their sleeves, others give a woman only the occasional glimpse," she commented dryly.

"Maybe there's some underlying fear? Ever think of

that? Clearly *I* can't wear my heart on my sleeve. I'm running this outfit."

"Don't worry. I've long since got the message."

"Have you *really*?" He flicked a diamond-hard glance at her. "Maybe you're not as good at interpreting as you think. Anyway, as a favour to me, don't give Rob the slightest encouragement. He doesn't need it."

"What, not even a smile?" Her blue eyes sparkled with challenge.

"Next thing you know he'll want to stay on longer." Keefe's answer was crisp.

"I don't think so," she disagreed. "There are lots of girls out there."

"Not like *you* there aren't," he clipped off. "Damn this thing!" He began to pull on the bandana around his neck to loosen it. They were all wearing protective bandanas. Hers was sapphire blue; Keefe's a bright red. The colour on him was wonderful, setting off the polished bronze of his skin.

She had never seen a man so impossibly dashing. "Anyway, it's like I said. I'm not going to compound your worries. I'm going home."

"Are you, Sky-Eyes?" He turned his dark head abruptly, pinning her gaze.

She took a quick fluttery breath. He hadn't called her *Sky-Eyes* since she couldn't remember when. "You know perfectly well I have to. You're my *fantasy* lover, Keefe," she said on a bitter-sweet note.

"Now you tell me. You dream of me." He looked straight ahead.

"Nightmares mostly." She laughed, but it came out off-key.

"But very *real*."

"*Very* real," she admitted, thinking of the torture of awakening to find he really wasn't there in the bed beside her.

"Even at their worst you want them," he said.

"One ought to be able to take medication for *want*."

"Maybe *want* is wired as much into the brain as the flesh." He broke off with a groan. "Look at Rachelle! Early morning isn't her scene. Why did she want to come?"

"Hopefully to see me take a tumble," she suggested, laconically.

"My sister is far more likely to be the one taking a tumble." His reply was grim.

"I hope not! Even under provocation I have no heart to wish any harm on Rachelle."

"Only on me."

"Don't be ridiculous, Keefe," she said sharply, rising above the difficulties that had been thrown in their way. "*You're* the person I'd miss most in the world. Not that you don't know it," she added, with a helpless flare of hostility.

He laughed beneath his breath, reaching across to lightly tap her hand. "Some things, Sky-Eyes, we can't change. Much as we fight it."

An hour later, the vast landscape was drenched in blazing sunlight. They cut a swathe through a section of Djinjara's great herd, which was moving in a slow, snake-like formation of well over a mile, undulating towards water. Riders surrounded the herd, keeping them in line with little effort. They exchanged waves. One of the aboriginal stockmen was giving voice to a native song not unlike a chant. Not only the cattle were finding the lilting sound calming, even though it had grown very hot by now. As always, they hoped for an afternoon thunderstorm to bring the blessed rain. Hope was everything on the desert fringe.

Jinjin was a moving mass of waterbirds, spoonbills, shags, white-faced herons with long pointed beaks, huge flocks of ibis. The pelicans wouldn't come into the swamps until they had good rains. Soaring red gums threw their long leafy arms over an amazing green carpet of lush grass with countless little wildflowers in all shades of purple. Their sweet fragrance was saturating the air. Obviously the whole amazing area was flourishing on the moisture drawn from beneath. It was alive with droning bees and dragonflies and multicoloured butterflies that drifted about like spent petals raining down from the trees.

"You'd swear the old guy knew we were after him," Keefe swept off his Akubra to savour a moment of cool relief

"Not here, boss," Jonah called. "Bin here, though. Ya can see all the tracks. Mebbe this mornin'. Can't be far."

"We'll take a ten-minute break," Keefe decided, already starting to dismount. Everyone was tired. So tired. But determined. There was a job to be done.

Skye followed suit. She was fading more quickly than she had thought. The shimmering heat over the spinifex plains was unholy. There was one plus, however. Her mare, with her thoroughbred lines and fine aristocratic head, was as smooth as silk to ride. That gave her extra confidence.

"This is awful!" Rachelle staggered up to them to complain. "I feel like I'm about to pass out." Her smooth olive skin was mottled with heat rash. Skye felt really sorry for her. No use to say, "You shouldn't have come, Rachelle." That would have been tantamount to waving a red flag in front of a bull.

Keefe looked at his sister with concern. "You wanted to come, Rachelle," he reminded her. "It *is* terribly hot. We're in for another dry storm. Why don't you relax for a while, cool down, then call it a day? We're over the worst of it, but there's more to come. The mob can't be far away."

Robert walked towards them, raising a hand. "It doesn't get much better than this," he enthused, his good-looking face aglow with heat and excitement. No brumby chases where he came from. No real rough and tumbles. "What a picturesque place!" he exclaimed. "It has to be seen to be believed. You couldn't even count the butterflies. But no brumbies, alas!"

"We'll find them," Keefe said with conviction.

"How's it going, Skye?" Robert transferred his gaze to Skye, thinking she looked a vision even after a tough ride. Her beautiful skin was flushed, honey-gold wisps of hair escaped from her thick plait to stray around her face: her eyes were as vivid a blue as the sky.

"Don't worry about *her,*" Rachelle broke in fiercely, obviously feeling very sorry for herself. "This is a real drag. I'll probably get stung by one of those damned bees." She swatted the golden-green air. "I could do with a cup of tea."

"Sorry. No tea," Keefe rose to his feet. "Tea later. We have to catch up with the mob. Old Man Mooki is onto us."

"Damn Old Man Mooki !" Rachelle cried out, in a fit of bad temper.

"Rachelle, I'm in no mood for mutiny." Keefe turned on his sister very quietly. "I understand you're tired. You've got right out of the way of things. We'll ride on, and you can head for home. Keep to the line of lagoons."

"I want Skye to come with me." Rachelle's dark glance veered from her brother to the silent, but sympathetic Skye.

"I'll come," Robert offered very gallantly when he was thoroughly enjoying the experience.

"I don't want *you,*" Rachelle announced rudely. "I want Skye."

"Only Skye's riding with me," Keefe told his sister, this time in a no-nonsense type of voice. "So is Rob. He's having a ball. You can easily find your way back, Rachelle. I can spare Eddie to go with you. Just take it nice and easy. Drink often from your water bottle."

"Thanks for nothing!" Rachelle cried hotly.

"It's yourself you have to blame." Briefly Keefe touched her shoulder. "Mount up now. The rest of us have to keep moving."

"Wait and see. I'll probably get sunstroke." Rachelle issued the dire warning. She had so hoped to see Skye drooping from exhaustion. No such luck.

"No, you wont," Keefe assured her. "You're carrying the McGovern banner."

CHAPTER FIVE

THEY finally caught up with the mob at a borehole. Roughly thirty wild horses, very tricky to catch. Old Man Mooki was the big black stallion that had run for years with his motley mob and ever-increasing harem, some of them mares he had taken from the station. Many attempts had been made to yard him in the past but Mooki had great legs, hence great speed. These days he wasn't as tough as he had been, but was still a formidable opponent.

"Let them drink their fill." From the shelter of the trees, Keefe issued the order just above his breath. "Slow 'em down. Then we'll try to drive them towards Yalla Creek. The bed is dry and the banks are steep. With any luck at all, the sand will wear them out."

Muscles tense, they awaited their moment.

Sharp old Mooki sensed them before they got anywhere near them. The colts threw up their heads as though at a signal. The mares began to snort and kick up. Next minute they were off, in a thunder of black, bay, piebald and chestnut bodies. They were moving so fast it seemed like they didn't have a hope in hell of catching them, Skye thought, hot on the chase. The mob, with Mooki in the lead, was doubling back towards the trees, unshod hooves pounding up a great billowing cloud of red dust, tangled manes and tails whipping in their own momentum.

They spread out, five of them now with Rachelle and Eddie out of the game. For the plan to succeed they had to head Mooki off. Turn him round. The mob would follow. It took nerve, but they forced themselves on, trying to ignore the heat of the day. Gradually the mares came down to a canter, one of the mares in foal dropping out of the race. The rest of the harem was slowing. Mooki and the colts were dead set to fight for their freedom. Keefe had plotted their course of action in advance. Yalla Creek wasn't all that far off. The sandy bed would prove heavy going for all the horses, including their own. The danger was that the youngsters in the mob would endeavour to get to the opposite side of the creek. The trick was not to give them the opportunity.

Keefe thundered past her, his bush shirt stuck to his back with sweat. He was taking chances, but he was a splendid horseman and his big gelding had endurance and a fabulous turn of speed.

Incredibly, out of nowhere a group of adult emus, standing nearly two metres high, decided to join in the chase. They must have felt threatened in some way because they put on a tremendous burst of speed—they were capable of sixty kilometres an hour—outrunning the tiring horses. It was a fantastic sight and would have been very funny if it hadn't been so dangerous to man and beast.

Heart in her throat, Skye found her second wind. She picked up her own speed, fanning out wide with Rob fanning away to her left. What if an emu decided to veer across their tracks? Years before a mounted stockman had been killed in a freak encounter with an irate emu protecting its nest. The only thing that surprised her was that a mob of kangaroos hadn't joined in. Give either species, just a hint of a chase and it was on!

Ahead Keefe and one of the stockmen had Mooki boxed in. Skye and Rob brought up the rear, with the remaining stockman going to their assistance. The brumby stallion was as good as penned. Only not to be outdone, Mooki took a mighty plunge into the creek, his hooves threshing about in the loose sand, his heaving sides lathered in sweat. A few of the colts hesitated, as though they knew they'd be bogged down in the sand, but the others followed their leader.

Inside ten minutes it was all over. The flightless emus, satisfied there was no threat being posed to them, trotted off sedately on their long grey legs. Keefe took his pick of the worn-out colts. The others, including the old war horse, Mooki, he let go.

"Really should shoot the ugly old thing!" Rob muttered. "He's a real pest."

"No need." Keefe would only shoot a horse when he absolutely had to. "Mooki is on his last legs. Have to hand it to him. He's a game old guy. What we have to do now is yard the colts. Not a bad bunch. We should be able to turn them into good working horses."

It turned out to be a hollow victory.

"I don't like the look of that sky." Keefe stared upwards with a frown on his brow. He had been sensing trouble for a while now. Familiar as they all were with the dry electrical storms, many times he found himself relying on a mix of intuition and experience for further developments. The mushrooming masses of steel-grey and black were almost directly overhead. It would be a miracle if there was rain in them. Still, the odd miracle did happen.

Thankfully they had finished constructing a makeshift holding yard, using stout coolabahs for posts. The colts had gone in quietly enough but now they were starting to mill about as glaring silver-blue flashes of lightning rent the heavens, followed by loud booms of thunder.

"Better take cover," Keefe shouted over the abruptly rising

wind. Their own horses were tied up securely. The stockmen set to arranging a tarpaulin as some sort of shelter. "Go on, Skye. Move it," Keefe ordered, over the howl of the wind. This was one time he wished she weren't there.

"You'd better move it too," she shouted back at him. "I don't like the look of this either." There could be a short sharp deluge, or the whole thing would pass yet again. It was those jagged lightning bolts that posed the danger.

"I'm not going to stand here arguing." Keefe seized her, easily gathering her up with one arm and sheltering her with his body. They made a race towards shelter but didn't make it before a lightning bolt, like a gigantic flashing mirror, shot down the sky like a missile and buried itself in the centre of the tallest gum. The strike was so bright it seared the eyes. Momentarily blinded, Skye felt Keefe's strong arm tighten to steel as he pitched her beneath the tarpaulin where she went sprawling on her hands and knees. Slightly winded, when she opened her eyes it was to see him turning back to free the penned colts.

The huge gum tree was still holding but fire was blossoming all over it so it stood like a towering armed statue alive with electric-blue flame.

The screams from the colts were horrifying; near human in terror, severely unsettling the station horses that were out of harm's way. Eddie had sprung to attention, going to Keefe's aid. Sooner or later the tree was going to explode. What then?

Skye started praying for a miracle.

Please bring on the rain.

She couldn't remain in the shelter. Surely they needed every pair of hands. Shakily she rose to her feet, feeling pain around her midriff where Keefe had grabbed her. Swiftly she made the judgment she would be best employed helping Rob tackle the far corner of the yard. Her bandana would have to act as a glove. She ripped it off, wrapping it tightly around her right hand. There wasn't a second to lose.

Keefe caught sight of her out of the corner of his eye. "I told you to keep back, Skye," he roared. "We'll handle it. Do what I tell you."

"I'll be okay!" she defied him, realising she was probably the only person on Djinjara who would dare to.

The truly bizarre thing was the wonderfully intoxicating smell of the burning tree.

"Hurry, Skye, we can do it!" Rob yelled to her, thrilled by her sheer guts. The heat was so intense they risked getting scorched but the focus was on freeing the wild horses.

She couldn't run away and hide. She had to face it. Do her bit.

Keefe's end of the makeshift yard predictably fell first, quickly followed by a general collapse. The terrified horses bolted out of the wrecked enclosure, galloping in a frenzy of fright for the open plain.

"Get to the gully." Keefe threw out an imperative hand, racing back to where the station horses were tethered. He untied the terrified animals, sending them on their way with a hard slap on the rump.

"Do you *ever* do what you're told?" Keefe got a fierce grip on Skye, half lifting her off the ground as they made a run for the gully, where he plunged them both in. It was from there, standing thigh deep in yellow brackish water, that they watched the gum tree come down with a mighty roar, sending up a billion sparks and a high, spiralling tongue of flame. That intoxicating smell of burning eucalyptus wood saturated the air.

Then came the smoke. Not good. That started them off coughing. Keefe buried Skye's head against his chest, his bush shirt sodden with gully water.

"Phew!" he exclaimed hoarsely. "I've never seen anything like that in my life."

Tentatively Skye lifted her head, her sensitive nostrils

flaring at a new scent on the air. Sulphur. "Keefe, I think it's going to rain," she said, wonder in her voice.

Keefe threw up his water-slicked dark head, his expression matching hers. "It is!" he said in amazement.

"Gosh, isn't that wonderful?" The moment seemed so ecstatic, words just bubbled up as if from an underground spring. "Want to kiss me?" she challenged, turning up her wet, glowing face.

"Do I!" He reached for her with tremendous urgency. The rain came pelting down… He continued to hold her, kissing her fiercely, never moving his mouth from hers. Mouths and bodies were fused wetly, unmistakably passionately together. They appeared to be oblivious to everyone and everything, even the rounds of clapping and the gleeful whoops!

Time to go home, Rob Sullivan thought, stunned by all he had witnessed. Now this! Keefe was a magnificent guy.

I guess he needs a magnificent woman.

The night before she was due to fly out of Djinjara on the first leg of her way home—Robert was heading back with her—Skye was invited up to the Big House for dinner. The invitation had been issued by Lady Margaret. She understood it had to be obeyed. She felt a violent tug of war on her emotions. She desperately wanted to be with Keefe before she left and she wanted to spend that last evening with her father.

"Go, love, go!" Jack expressed his encouragement. "Lady McGovern thinks the world of you." He paused for a telling moment. "So does Keefe."

"The kiss got around?" Skye faced her father across the table.

"Yeah, well, what did you expect, love? We all know you and Keefe share a bond. I sort of thought of it as…affection?"

He sounded worried, Skye thought. How had he missed her real feelings for Keefe? He was her father after all. Or had he deliberately chosen to hide from what had been right under his nose? Damaged people did. "You have a problem with me kissing Keefe, Dad?" she prompted, fully aware her father was a man who, in his own words, "kept his place". Was he worried that he could possibly lose his job as a result of this new development?

"Problem?" Jack's expression suddenly relaxed. "As I heard it, he grabbed *you*!"

Skye reached for his hand. Now wasn't the right moment to confide in him. "It was just one of those things. You know how it is. The rain coming down at that precise moment was fantastic. Like a gift from Heaven. It put out the fire."

"Still, a *kiss*?" Jack, not to be put off, searched her eyes.

"A kiss, Dad. That's all."

Jack scoffed. "A single kiss can change a life. I should know. So how is this kiss going to affect everyone at the house? I reckon you ought to prepare yourself for some attack from Rachelle. By the way, Scott's girlfriend turned up this afternoon when you were out taking photographs."

She nodded. "I noticed a plane fly over when I was taking shots of Manguri." She referred to Djinjara's revered desert monument. "By Scott's girlfriend, you mean Jemma Templeton?"

Jack nodded. "That's the word. Plain girl, but very sweet and gracious. Too good for Scott, I fear. He won't be faithful."

"I expect not," Skye sighed. "You think they'll make a match of it?"

"I'm more interested in what's going on between you and Keefe." Jack continued to study Skye's face. "It seems to me in a perfect world, you'd be perfect for each other. But in the *real* world there's me, your dad. Plain old Jack McCory, station overseer, a man who had to leave school at fourteen. You can take your place anywhere, you're a beautiful, educated woman, but I'm just good old Jack. Are you anxious about that, love?"

Skye's tender heart melted. "How could I possibly be anxious about you, Dad? I love you. Never mind with the McGoverns. Anyway, Keefe thinks very highly of you. You wouldn't be overseer if you couldn't handle everything that's thrown at you."

"True." Jack felt quite secure in his own capabilities as Djinjara's overseer. "But *socially*, I mean. The McGoverns are Outback royalty. We both know that. Look at it from the family's point of view."

"You're jumping too far ahead, Dad." She strove to slow him down, though she herself was concerned about the McGovern's reactions.

"If Keefe kissed you—in front of everyone—it means he couldn't care less about what anyone thinks," Jack reasoned. "I see it as the equivalent of a commitment. Especially from Keefe. It wouldn't mean much coming from Scott, but Keefe is something else again."

"I can't argue with that," she said quietly. "But I'm sure the family is expecting Keefe to do a whole lot better than me. Best to face it squarely, Dad."

"Damn it all, he *couldn't* do better," Jack stoutly maintained. "But we both know the McGovern clan are first-class snobs. That Rachelle has given you hell over the years."

Skye sighed. "She has in her way, but it's not so much snobbery, Dad. Rachelle has convinced herself I robbed her of her brother's affection. It's not true, but that's the way she feels. She doesn't have a lot of insight into her own behaviour."

"Have you and Keefe come to any sort of agreement?" Jack asked tentatively. "You don't have to tell me if you don't want to. At least, not until there's something to say."

"There's nothing *to* say, Dad." She shook her head. "Keefe and I have always shared a strong bond but we haven't moved on. There are all sorts of difficulties."

"I can see something is weighing heavily on your mind.

Don't worry, I won't ask. I'll wait for you to tell me. You're the best daughter in the world." He covered her hand with his own.

Jack drove her up to the house at seven sharp. She had anticipated being asked to dinner at least once so she had packed a pair of black evening trousers worn with a simple black top with a sapphire-blue satin trim. She clipped on silver earrings and a rather lovely silver cuff. Black high heels and she was ready to present herself for McGovern inspection. She had learned Jemma's parents had arrived with her. The father, Farleigh Templeton, had been piloting his Beech Baron.

Keefe was waiting for her in the hallway. Immediately she felt that manic upsurge in her blood. It was hell to be so passionately in love with him. She should stay away from him entirely.

You can't do that. He's in your blood.

And there it was again. The question of *blood*.

"You look beautiful, very *chic*!" His brilliant gaze flared over her, taking in every last detail.

The pride in his voice made her heart ache. How had she found the strength to deny him when he had wanted her? Yet she had. There was such a cloud hanging over them.

"You know the Templetons are here?" He took her arm, his long fingers a caress.

"Dad told me. Maybe they want to put a bit of pressure on Scott?" she suggested.

"I wonder if that would be wise." Keefe's expression went wry. "Right now I can't think Scott would make a good husband. He has a bit of maturing to do."

"How would you rate yourself as a potential husband?" She gave him a sideways glance.

"What a question!"

"Maybe you can't or won't bring the same singularity of purpose you apply to everything else to settling on the right woman."

"Stop it, Skye," he warned, catching her hand and pressing his thumb into the palm. "God, I wish you weren't going back tomorrow."

"I must." Just his thumb working her palm, yet the movement radiated sexuality. Her entire body was aquiver. "There's bound to be something pressing to claim me. By the way, you'd best tell me now. Has Rob given the family the tip-off about our unpremeditated kiss?"

"To my knowledge Rob hasn't said a word," Keefe said. "And really, Skye-Eyes, that had to be one of the best kisses of all time."

"Agreed." She couldn't help but smile. "But you took a risk. The news has flown around. Dad spoke to me about it. I would say he's concerned."

"About what, exactly?" Keefe asked coolly. "You've learned nothing from him about your mother?"

"My mother was Dad's mystery woman, Keefe."

"Was there *nothing* he asked her?"

"Seems not." She shrugged wryly. "Dad deemed it a miracle when my mother said she would marry him."

"Not much of a courtship," he said bluntly.

Skye came to a halt, her eyes a blue flame. "Dad's love for my mother was *real.*"

"I don't doubt it." Keefe spoke with a mixture of frustration and impatience. "I'll pick my moment carefully to speak to Gran. I suppose an interrogation is what it amounts to. Even if we *are* related in some way—it seems we're both enmeshed in that one—it can't be all that close."

"Yet we've always had feelings for one another, haven't we? Strong feelings. A strong bond."

His lean fingers tightened around her arm. "So what does that prove?" He offered it like a challenge.

"It proves there's a strong possibility cracks in our relationship might open up."

* * *

They were all assembled in the very English-looking drawing room, the huge area divided by a splendid triple arch and lit by two magnificent matching Waterford crystal chandeliers. Insolent Scott and a smiling Farleigh Templeton stood in front of the white marble fireplace, filled for most of the year with a variety of lush indoor plants and blossoming branches. Over the mantel hung an enormous rectangular, very important-looking Georgian mirror, reflecting the backs of the heads of the two tall men.

There was no shortage of serious antiques in the Big House, Skye thought wryly. Yet they mingled happily with more exotic items from India and the Orient. Lady McGovern herself had until fairly recent times been a great collector of just about everything: paintings—one would have thought they had enough—porcelain; beautiful pieces of furniture; exquisite rugs. And books. Lady McGovern loved books. They were stacked on just about every table. Skye, a book lover herself, had absolutely no argument with that. She only wished she could grab a few. She spotted Margot Fonteyn's biography side by side with Robert Helpmann's on the library table in the entrance hall as they had come in.

Rachelle had cornered Rob, who was looking more than a little rattled. A youthful-looking Meredith Templeton, far better endowed than her daughter in the looks department, was in the midst of an animated conversation with Lady McGovern, with Jemma looking quietly on. They all broke off to stare at Skye as she entered the room with the Master of Djinjara.

The two of them seen together were stunning. Perfect foils for each other, Lady McGovern thought. Keefe so dark of hair and bronzed of complexion; Skye the blue-eyed, golden-honey blonde. Skye, being Skye, was giving no thought to the impact of her own beauty, unaware she was catching all the light. Of course they had all heard versions of that burning kiss. She, for one, heard *everything* that went on at the vast station. Some things she wouldn't tell. Things that were secreted in her heart. Not that she had one hundred per cent proof. Just the awful nagging anxiety that had never left her. The bond between Skye and her beloved grandson forged in childhood had reached the dangerous stage.

Such a shame, a shame, a terrible shame... Both would be badly wounded. That's if it was the truth. Lady McGovern took turns at belief and disbelief. Too fearful of going further. Lives could be destroyed. But knowing her grandson as she did, she knew he wouldn't rest until he had the truth by the throat. Her unwillingness to speak of the past—the secrets she had buried—she accepted now would have to be revealed with all their wider implications. Not only Keefe and Skye would be devastated. What about Jack? Sometimes nothing was as it appeared to be. Sometimes the truth destroyed.

Dinner was over. Skye walked with Keefe through the home gardens, under palm fronds and low-arching branches freighted with summer blossom. Above them a glorious starred sky: Orion, the mighty hunter, Alpha, Centauri, Sirius, watchdog of the night sky, the sparkling river of diamonds, Lilah Lilya, the Milky Way, and burning bright over the sand-hills the five points of Jirranjoonga, the Southern Cross. Around them a wonderfully scented desert landscape. They might have been inside a bush cathedral. Silently, as though locked in their own thoughts, they reached one of the pavilions that had been built at various points around the extensive grounds. This one, hexagonal in structure, featured white trelliswork that supported a prolifically flowering king jasmine. After the intense heat of the day, the desert quickly cooled off, so the air was sublimely fresh.

Without a word, Keefe put his strong hands to her slender

hips, trapping her against him. "Alone at last!" His striking face bore an expression that held both hunger and pain.

She sighed deeply as an answering emotion engulfed her. Sensually she leaned into him. So thrilling! "Did you see their faces?"

"Okay." He drew back, a faint edge to his voice, knowing his family had heard about the kiss. "I saw their faces. But I thought dinner went well. The Templetons are very pleasant people."

"They are. Even so, it was easy to gauge everyone's surprise. Correction—make that shock."

"Who would care?" he said impatiently. "There couldn't be a woman on earth who makes me feel like you do. Come closer to me, Skye. I can't seem to get you close enough.'

Unable to help herself, she fitted herself against him. They were a perfect physical match. "This is what it comes to in the end, isn't it?" she asked poignantly. "We need to make love."

"Evidently I want it more than you do," he told her with a twisted smile.

"I wouldn't be too sure of that." She turned her head this way and that so he could nuzzle her neck. Impossible to *think* when her whole body was transformed into a column of sensation.

"What bothered me more was the way Scott kept directing looks your way." He lifted his head abruptly to search her face.

So Scott had. Looks that had made her feel she needed to protect herself. But she couldn't tell Keefe that. Thwarted desire only too often turned to hate. "People don't change," she said very quietly.

"He won't bother you." His vibrant voice held a distinct rasp.

"He can scarcely do that as I'm going home."

"So you keep saying." He pressed his mouth to the sensitive spot beneath her ear. Not content, he slipped off her earring and put it in his pocket. Then he returned to teasing and gently nipping the lobe. "I thought Djinjara was your home?" he muttered. "I detest these separations."

She gave a little discordant laugh. "Just think, if we were anywhere else—in the city instead of on Djinjara—I suppose I could be your mistress?" There was just a glimmer of goading in her voice. "Your sister finds it *unthinkable* you could fall in love with me. Your grandmother too looked very watchful. She's fond of me but I definitely don't figure in her plans."

He broke off his ministrations, stepping out of the role of lover. "Much as I love Gran, I make my own plans," he said firmly. "You ought to know that."

"Then what are we *doing*, Keefe?" She sought an answer.

"Could you forget me?" he countered with intensity.

"Sometimes I wish I could," she burst out emotionally. "Sometimes—"

"Sometimes, sometimes...do you how much I ache for you?" Keefe lowered his head, covered her mouth so effectively it cut off her breath.

He kissed her until she was whimpering, desperate to fall into his bed.

"This is torture," he muttered. He was speaking for both of them. His tongue parted her lips again, making urgent contact with the slickness within. It was an intense encounter. No time for tenderness. Only raw passion, made more ravenous by the prospect of being parted. He was holding her so powerfully, her juddering back was arched against the vine covered trellis. It was *insane*—someone might come—but she was letting herself simply melt. His hand, imperceptibly trembling, had pushed down into her low-necked top, his fingers finding her already swollen nipple, working it and her into an erotic frenzy. She could feel his hard arousal. Her own core had long since gone liquid in response.

One of his long legs drove hers apart. They strained ever closer with the primitive desire to be naked. However lightly she was dressed, Skye felt her clothing to be as restrictive as a spacesuit. There was only one end to this kind of love-making. Where they were and who they were was all but obliterated by a consuming passion. Such was the level of intensity she wanted to tear at his clothes, press her mouth against his naked chest. Her hand moved to the buttons of his shirt. She wanted skin, not fabric.

"Someone is coming," he muttered in her ear. Even then he had to say it twice.

"Oh!" She strained to hear. Then the sound of a too-familiar voice, "They must be around here somewhere."

Skye forced herself to move. She was having difficulty trying to regulate her breathing. Only Keefe, in a gesture that wasn't at all hurried, clasped her arm. "Sometimes I love my sister. Other times I loathe her. Let's get out of here before she moves in on us."

A few minutes later Rachelle, hot on the trail, followed by a reluctant and embarrassed Jemma and a silent Scott, found them strolling companionably along the wooden bridge that spanned the lily pool. There was nothing in their demeanour to suggest this wasn't simply a friendly after-dinner stroll yet when Keefe turned to answer a question from Jemma—something to do with the water-lilies—Scott seized the opportunity to move too close to Skye's side.

In the darkness his hand trailed insolently down over her back. He took the insult a step further, pressing his fingers into the sides of her breasts. "I bet you two have had it off," he whispered in her ear, taking advantage of the cover afforded by Rachelle's over-loud voice. "Didn't want *me*, though, did you?" he muttered. "Only Keefe would do. But that's *all* you are to him, sweetheart, a groundsheet."

It was an outpouring of jealousy and venom. On the verge of slapping his face with all her might, Skye brought herself under control. "I pity poor Jemma," she muttered with the utmost contempt, spinning to face him. "You're a pig!"

It was an insult but from the smile on Scott's face he appeared to enjoy it.

Indeed, Scott was thinking there was no reason why he shouldn't give Skye hell. His strong attraction to her had never wavered. It leapt to a consistent high every time he laid eyes on her. It seemed entirely reasonable to him that if a man wasn't allowed to love a woman, he might as well do an about-face and hate her. After all love and hate were but two sides of the same coin. Her beauty alone charged his anger. How in hell was he supposed to marry poor old Jemma? She was as prim as a convent-trained schoolgirl. No excitement there. No extravagant desire. Just a dreary safe match. He wouldn't even consider it only Jemma would bring with her a handsome dowry. What had he to lose really? Jemma would love him no matter what he did. And he fully intended to do as he pleased. She was a fool to trust him. But, then, she was the sort of woman who could blind herself to the foibles of the man she loved.

At this point, Scott's complex feelings towards his brother turned savage. He was shot through with envy. Why should *Keefe* get everything he wanted? Why should Keefe get Skye? There was something in the McCorys' background that needed to be investigated. Some kind of crisis involving Skye's mother. He had always assumed Jack McCory had got her pregnant, thereby forcing a marriage. Why else would she have married him? She had been a lady from all accounts. What the hell was Jack McCory? A stockman on the lowest rung of the ladder. How had Gran allowed it? He had never heard his grandmother mention let alone discuss Catherine McCory in his entire life. Yet Catherine McCory had been buried in the McGovern graveyard.

There had to be a reason. All of a sudden Scott was determined on knowing what.

CHAPTER SIX

LADY MARGARET MCGOVERN was sitting in front of her triple-mirrored dressing table, staring sightlessly at her own reflection. It revealed a deeply troubled eighty-year-old woman whose features still bore the vestiges of great beauty. Lady Margaret was waiting for her beloved grandson Keefe to join her. She dreaded the thought of anyone overhearing their discussion. Rachelle wasn't above eavesdropping. Neither, for that matter, was Scott, but they were downstairs with Jemma and her parents, playing cards. Rachelle adored card games and she was a very good chess player. Lady Margaret knew full well the Templetons and, of course, Jemma herself had their hearts set on a match with Scott. They had made that perfectly plain. Lady Margaret had wanted—had indeed tried—to speak to Jemma. To warn her? But she despaired of Jemma now. That young woman would be deaf to anything in the least negative she had to say about Scott. She was convinced Jemma knew in her heart that married life with Scott would be far from easy, but it was obvious Jemma preferred to be miserable with Scott than happy with anyone else.

So there it was! A marriage that would somehow endure or inevitably crash. Only time would tell.

This conversation with Keefe had to be kept entirely confidential. That was why it was being conducted in the privacy of her bedroom. Not that she planned to initiate anything. She would wait on Keefe's questions, then try to steer a safe course through a sea littered with icebergs. Nothing much in Cathy's background to be worried about. Her personal history was something else again. Stick with the background. The wonder of it was she hadn't been called to account long before this. Such a heavy burden! She would be glad to lay it down. Keeping secrets was a curse.

Keefe knocked on the door then entered on his grandmother's summons.

He had to smile. It was as much a command as a simple response to his knock. As long as he could remember, his grandmother had been very much in command. Keefe opened the door into the richly furnished bedroom, with its canopied bed, antique furnishings and fine paintings. The sitting room, equally opulent, was to one side, dressing room, bathroom to the other. His grandmother was seated in a splendid gilt armchair, one of a pair she and his grandfather had bought at a Christie's auction many years before. The antiques had all but taken over, he thought. But his grandmother had always indulged her passion for collecting. Perhaps to a fault.

She was still wearing the violet silk dress she had worn at dinner but she had taken off her double string of perfectly matched pearls. They were so big that on someone else—outside Royalty—they would have been mistaken for costume jewellery. Not so his grandmother.

The expression on her face was mask-like as usual, but he knew the mask covered a seething cauldron of emotions. Either way it rent his heart. He loved his grandmother, even if he was aware of her manipulative qualities and secretive nature. She had such *presence.*

"Sit down, dear," she said, indicating the other chair with a graceful wave of her hand.

Keefe laughed. "I think I'll take the sofa, Gran. I'd hate to break one of those gilded legs.'

"Don't be silly, darling," she chided. "Your grandfather used to sit in them. Your grandfather bought them, for that matter. For me, of course."

"A lot of years have gone by since then, I think." Keefe chose to lower his six-foot-plus frame onto the sofa, which was covered in a beautiful, white patterned blue silk. "You look tense, Gran," he began, knowing a moment of anxiety and regret that this conversation had to come about. Since his father's death his grandmother, a permanent fixture in his life, was looking decidedly frail. "I don't want to worry you or cause you upset, but there are some things I need to know."

"You love Skye?" Lady McGovern cut to the heart of it.

He had no intention of denying it. That would be a betrayal of the woman he loved. "I've always loved her. You must know that. I loved her when we were kids. I'm madly in love with Skye, the woman. She's everything I want."

"So what is it you wish to know?"

The question was asked in such a way there couldn't have been a thing in Skye's background that wouldn't bear scrutiny.

Keefe's striking features grew tight with controlled anger. Here it was again. The long-maintained silence; the stone-walling, what had to be a cover-up. "I want to know all about Skye's mother's background," he said in a quiet voice that nevertheless demanded she listen. "I want, Skye wants—and her wants are more important than mine—some kind of resolution on this. The not knowing is impacting heavily on our relationship. You were obviously very attached to Skye's mother. It was on your say-so she was buried in the family cemetery. No one outside the family ever has been accorded that privilege—call it what you like."

"*Privilege* is what *I* call it," Lady McGovern said severely, attempting to hide her trepidation behind matriarchal power.

She knew it wouldn't work with Keefe. He was Master of Djinjara now. She was the McGovern dowager.

"Tell me who Catherine McCory really was. The little you've revealed over the years just isn't so. She's never been spoken about within the family. Dad, to my knowledge, rarely mentioned her, yet he was very kind to Skye.'

"Who wouldn't be?" Lady McGovern raised her thinly arched brows.

"She *was* related to you, wasn't she? Come out with it, Gran. We've all taken that on board. Was her maiden name really Newman? So far we have been able to find a record of a Catherine Newman entering the country from the UK for two years before she first came to visit."

"We? You and Skye have been checking?" Lady McGovern's expression turned steely.

"*I* have someone on it, Gran." He cut her short. "I can't allow you to override the fact I love Skye. I want to marry her but I need to be able to think ahead."

"Dear God!" Lady McGovern threw up her hands in horror. "How could you betray *family*, Keefe? I don't believe it!"

"With all due respect, Gran, you might be the one who's been doing that," he retorted bluntly. "It hasn't been easy to go behind your back but you, yourself, are the cause of that. Would you answer the question please? What *is* the mystery? Was Catherine sent out here because of a certain incident, her behaviour perhaps? Could she have been a little wild in her youth? She was dead at twenty-two. She appeared to have had no one. No family. It's as if she didn't belong anywhere. You took charge of her. I want to know why. I believe it's your duty to tell me. Skye certainly has a right to know. Far from investigating, Skye actually fears delving into her mother's background. You must know that. It's an instinctive thing, call it intuition. For the past couple of years Skye has been full of unease. So have I. But why *unease* exactly? Both of us have it in our heads we're somehow related. It has stopped us from going forward. But it couldn't be *close* surely, so what's the problem? Now's your time to tell me. Put certain issues to rest. I can't lose Skye. I can't allow her to move away from me. It's not on. So tell me, what brought Catherine to Australia? What brought her to *you*? Djinjara is the McGovern spiritual and ancestral home, but it's just about as remote as a young girl could get from a home in England. I should warn you to tell the truth. A lot rides on it."

"Warn me?" Lady McGovern stared back at her grandson in shock.

"Yes, warn you, Gran," he confirmed quietly, taking her thin trembling hand. "I fully intend to marry Skye, but not until this matter is cleared up. Can't you see both of us need reassurance, Skye most of all? The mystery if there is one, needs to be solved. I need to set her mind at rest. I can't imagine for the life of me why there has *been* all this mystery surrounding Catherine Newman. I need enlightenment right now."

"Neumann," Lady McGovern corrected, looking away from her grandson's dynamic face. "Katrina Neumann. Katrina was a wild child. She was the daughter of a dear childhood friend of mine, Leonora Werner. We went to school together. I often vacationed at Leonora's beautiful family manor as a girl. We were playing in the garden when we overheard a conversation between Leonora's mother, Iona, and her husband, Axel. Axel was accusing Iona of being unfaithful to him. Leonora wasn't his child. Previously he had doted on her and Leonora on him. Lord knows, Axel Werner had many an affair himself, but there again the double standard. He was quite the playboy, very blond, blue eyed, very handsome, German born. Leonora's mother swore that whoever had told him such a thing was out for some kind of sick revenge. Perhaps one of *his* lovers?"

"That must have been terrible for your friend." Keefe frowned, trying to process all this unexpected information.

"Terrible for us both, but naturally Leonora felt the shock most violently. We ran away as fast as we could. We had to stop when she was became ill. I could only kneel and hold her head while she retched her heart out. That was the start of it all. Leonora's parents separated soon after that, divorced. Leonora wasn't mentioned in her *father's* will, although she was an only child. She never contested it, believing herself to be illegitimate. Who knows, maybe she was? One wouldn't like to count the number of cases where the husband isn't the biological father. I promised Leonora when she was dying that Katrina would have safe haven with me if she was ever in need of it. Iona blamed Leonora, shockingly unfairly, for the break-up of her marriage. Leonora left home at age seventeen, she'd been at boarding school with me most of the time. She and her mother never spoke again."

Keefe shook his head incredulously. "It's a sad story, Gran, but it hardly warrants all this secrecy. Unless Skye's mother came to you pregnant with no place to turn?"

"No, no!" Margaret McGovern vigorously shook her pure white head.

"I'm asking you again, Gran," he said tautly, wanting to keep her on track.

"Katrina wanted to put half the world between herself and the past." Lady McGovern was showing her agitation. "She came on her own to Australia. She knew about me, of course, from her mother. It took great courage what she did. She could have had a splendid life. Personally I believe Leonora *was* Axel's child. Axel was very blond, blue eyed. But then so was Leonora, Iona and Katrina," she sighed. "The look and the colouring passed to Skye. I used to think I saw a resemblance to Axel Werner in my friend. Even in Skye."

"DNA could have solved it but then it wasn't available in those days." Keefe frowned.

"Good enough reason for a lot of women to fear it now it

is," Lady McGovern shot back, her tone harsh. She began to flex her arthritic fingers.

"So what you're saying is at some time Katrina aka Catherine met Jack McCory, who is still a fine-looking man, fell in love with him, maybe became pregnant before they got around to getting married. Is that it? Lift your head, please, Gran. I can't see your eyes."

Lady McGovern felt like she was suffocating, a pillow held over her head. Airless, struggling for breath, she answered, "I've always believed Katrina married Jack McCory when she found herself pregnant. What has caused me endless trauma over these long years is that I don't believe Jack is Skye's father."

A deadly silence filled up the opulent room.

Keefe sprang up from the sofa, a man pole-axed. *"Dear God!"* His exclamation of shock resounded like a rifle shot.

"I can't bear to say it again," Lady McGovern told him, very piteously for her.

"Then who, Gran?" Keefe at that moment was laying full blame on his grandmother's shoulders. "Put a name to your fears. But be very, very careful. My father was a great man. He was a married man. Maybe his marriage didn't work out the way he hoped, but he was no adulterer."

Lady McGovern blinked rapidly. "What are you saying, Keefe?" Her tone soared. "What are you thinking? Your father, Broderick, never! Please calm yourself."

"I'm calm enough," he retorted angrily. "I repeat. Who?" Keefe, realising he was shouting, reined himself in.

Lady McGovern drew a long quavering breath. "Jonty," she managed at long last. "My dead son, Jonty. Your Uncle Jonathon.

As a revelation it had never crossed Keefe's mind. He slumped back onto the sofa, holding his head in his two hands. "Uncle Jonty?" he asked in patent disbelief. Uncle Jonty, who had taken a fatal crash off his motorbike while rounding up a few head of cattle. Uncle Jonty, who had died at roughly the same age as Katrina Neumann.

Lady McGovern looked across at her splendid grandson, seeing his tremendous shock. "I could be wrong," she said, very timidly. "But they fell in love."

Keefe felt the tension in every knotted muscle of his body. "God, Gran! We've been focusing on Catherine and all along you've been worrying yourself sick thinking Uncle Jonathon could have been the father of Katrina's child. Which would make Skye my first cousin."

"Exactly." Lady McGovern drew a jagged breath, wondering if she was about to have a panic attack. "Of course, first cousins have married, but—"

"A damned big *but*!" Keefe cried, making no excuse for swearing in front of his grandmother, something he had never done. Skye would be horrified. She could even call a halt to their relationship, even if he already knew he was prepared to go ahead. *No matter what.* His mind was working furiously. He wasn't exactly certain but he was pretty sure there was no legal or moral impediment to first cousins marrying. If his grandmother's revelation was true, he knew in his heart it would have a devastating impact on Skye. And Jack. No getting away from it! "Stop there, Gran," he said with the voice of command. "Just stop. I need time to take this all in."

Right outside Lady McGovern's door, one ear pressed against the woodwork, a third party stood and listened. Keefe's voice, deep and resonant, carried at any time. When he shouted— he did so rarely, no need to when everyone stood to attention—the sound carried into the carpeted hallway.

So Skye McCory was a close relative after all! That was enough to break up any family. Enough to break up a passionate love affair. This piece of information, which had come as just as much of a shock as it had to Keefe, cried aloud to be used…

* * *

Skye spent all morning in court. She was seated just behind Derrick Sellway, a big blond handsome thirty-five-year-old man in an expensive dark suit. Derrick was the barrister representing her client. She had done her job to the best of her ability, assembling all the information necessary for Derrick to plead their client's case and hopefully win her a fairer deal. This was a particularly messy fight over money. Not big money as money went, but rather an unholy war between a brother and sister who had gained far bigger legacies from their late father's estate, and the other sister, much younger than the other two, their client, presenting her case to the court for a fairer deal. The brother and elder sister were prosperous people very much acting together. The younger sister had come through a sad divorce and had been left holding the children, in her case twins. She had had a falling-out with her father over her choice of a husband. But now the husband was gone. Literally fled overseas. Their client's circumstances had been considerably reduced. Skye thought she had done enough background checking on the brother and elder sister. In her view—and she hoped in the view of the court—a whole lot of undue influencing had gone on with the ailing father, obviously in an effort to gain, if not the entire estate, the lion's share.

Derrick was doing a fine job of presenting the facts to the court. He had just the right appearance and a fine, persuasive speaking voice. She had high hopes for her client, who was trying to pick up the pieces of her shattered life. Skye genuinely liked and admired her. Now it came down to what the court thought…

The afternoon was spent at a community legal centre where she did pro bono work from time to time. The numbers of women in distress; the numbers who couldn't afford legal representation! The case she had elected to take on was just another in a long line of domestic abuse cases. She wouldn't have any difficulty obtaining a restraining order against the husband, even though she knew only too well some men didn't know the meaning of the word "restraint". Such men picked their victims. Her client, a pretty, vulnerable woman with very low self-esteem and badly hurting, was just as likely to return to the abusive marriage no matter how much counselling and free representation she received. That was the sad part. Still, one had to try. The bravest fought free if only for the sake of their children. Even then, no one was assured of a good outcome. There was terrible danger in making an enemy of a violent man.

It was well after six when she drove into the underground parking area of her apartment complex. She had cancelled a work-related function. That upset Derrick, the high flyer, who appeared to have settled on her, quite without encouragement, as a suitable wife. Both of them were lawyers. They had much in common, except, on Skye's side, love. Derrick was attractive, clever and dryly amusing, inclined to be pompous but able to take a joke against himself. They had spent a good bit of time together one way or another. The only thing wrong: he wasn't Keefe. There was only one Keefe. Nothing could change that.

Inside her apartment she went about switching on a few lights, taking pleasure in her surroundings. After a lifetime with the McGoverns, having access to the Big House with all its splendid furnishings, she had acquired "taste without the big bucks", as a friend had once said. She had been admiring Skye's latest acquisition—a large abstract canvas titled *Purple Haze*—at the time, a surreal sky, line of hills, boulders tumbling down it into the highly swelling waves of the dark blue sea. Was that a sea-tossed small boat in the middle? She thought so. The sea reflected in just the right spots the purples, pinks and amethysts of the sky. The artist was young, clearly very gifted, but not as yet in a position to ask big money. Even so, it hadn't been cheap, neither would she have expected it to be. The painting looked stunning on the living-room wall. It was mounted above the three-seater sofa and matching armchairs. The colours she loved prevailed in the room, the blues and golden hues, the accents of lime green and amethyst.

It occurred to her she was hungry. She had been constantly on the go, missing lunch with only a welcome cup of tea and a biscuit at the community centre. Swiftly she changed out of her smart grey business suit worn with a blue silk blouse, hanging it up before pulling a loose caftan over her head. On the job she usually wore her long thick mane pulled back from her face in some way. Now she pulled the pins out of her updated knot, setting her hair free. A nice cold glass of Sauvignon Blanc would go down well. Maybe smoked salmon and scrambled eggs, a green salad? She only wanted something light.

Just as she was pouring the wine, she was surprised by the sound of the buzzer on her security video unit. Who could be buzzing her at this time of the evening? Whoever it was, she intended to answer or ignore the call, depending on who showed up on the brightly coloured screen. She paused, put down her wineglass then went to check the video picture.

At first she couldn't make out who it was, he was so tall. In the next second the man's head came into focus as he moved nearer the security door.

It was Keefe! She pushed the talk button, saying breathlessly, "Come up." She pressed the unlock button, glancing around quickly. All was in order. Her blue caftan was a bit see-through, but this was Keefe after all. He knew every inch, every curve, of her body. But what was he doing here? Why hadn't he let her know he was coming into town? It was almost too much excitement to handle. Her heart was beating in double time. Was he here on McGovern business, or had he brought her some kind of news? Thrilled as she was by his totally unexpected visit, she sagged back against the wall. No rationality to it, just an intuitive sense that something could be wrong. She couldn't think further…

When she opened the door to Keefe she felt the same electric jolt she always felt at the sight of him. She stepped right into his outstretched arms. He held her with one arm around the waist, shutting the weighted door after him. He didn't speak. Instead, he lowered his head to kiss her with passionate intensity, gathering up her body and holding it close against his as though her satiny woman's flesh possessed some special magic for him.

"You're here?" She showed her surprise when at last they pulled apart.

"Sorry I didn't let you know." His brilliant eyes saw through to her inner trepidation.

"That's okay." She drew him by one hand into the living room. "It's wonderful to see you. That's if you're *real*." She turned back to soak in the sight of him. He always looked sublimely handsome to her eyes; the beautiful dominant male, his expression brooding, which struck her as also romantic, his aura beyond compelling. He was wearing street clothes, a fitted casual jacket over designer jeans, an open-necked white cotton shirt with fine multi-stripes beneath. This was the first time he had ever been in her apartment, and she saw him take a quick, enveloping look around.

"Your sanctuary from the world?"

"Like it?" she asked.

He inclined his dark head. "You've got great taste in everything." He walked towards *Purple Haze*. "This makes quite a statement," he said. "Is it a boat out there in that spectacular ultramarine sea?"

"*I* think so. I'm glad you do too. Would you like a glass of wine? I've just opened a bottle of Sauvignon Blanc."

"A Scotch would be better if you've got it," he said, shouldering out of his jacket and placing it over the back of a Chinese chair. Next he rolled back the long sleeves of his shirt to the elbow, the gold Rolex on his left wrist gleaming in the light.

"One Scotch coming up. I always keep a bottle on hand. Don't like it myself."

"But the odd colleague or two does?" He turned back to look at her. The overhead lighting in the galley kitchen was turning her hair to spun gold. It glanced off the gauze of her long dress, the contours of her beautiful breasts, clear to his gaze. His need for her; his *desire* was incurable. He wondered if such a powerful connection was rare.

"Actually, it's a female colleague of mine who can really knock it back." She laughed. "Ice?"

"Just a cube or two." Hands thrust into the pockets of his jeans, he walked slowly towards a set of four desert photographs she'd had framed and hung—two up, two down—on the end wall. "You're an artist yourself. These are very good. You shot them on Djinjara."

He knew his land. "My impressions," she said. "I love photography. I love it even better than practising law. There's so much heartache in what I do. So much I can't prevent."

"I can imagine." He paused a breath away from her, inhaling her fragrance. "We're going to have a talk, Sky-Eyes."

"I thought so." Now she gave vent to a troubled sigh. "You've spoken to your grandmother?"

"I said I would."

His expression was enigmatic. "So what did you find out?" She set about pouring a measure of single malt Scotch into a crystal tumbler, aware of her trembling hand. She walked to the refrigerator to release two ice cubes from the dispenser on the door. Playing for time. Her heart was hammering in her breast.

"Come and sit down." He took the tumbler from her. "You

look magical. I'm reminded of the way Jack always called your mother his princess. I *love* the dress."

"Caftan." She tried to smile, but butterflies were flitting madly about in her stomach "I usually slip into something light when I'm on my own." She curled herself into one corner of the sofa, watching him take a quick swallow of whisky. "Tell me, whatever it is." Following his lead, she sipped her citrus-scented wine, then set her glass down on the long red-laquered Chinese chest she used as a sofa table.

Keefe told her what he knew. Up to a point. The question of her paternity he held back. He feared her reaction. He could see she was already reeling with shock.

"So my mother's name was really Katrina Neumann? But that's a German name."

"A strong German connection," he confirmed. "Your great-grandfather Axel Werner was German born. Perhaps the Neumanns were involved with Werner in business."

"And Dad was so infatuated, so far gone, he made my mother pregnant?" she asked in disbelief. "It could have been a disaster. I don't believe Dad would have let himself do that. Not before marriage. I mean, it was such a risky relationship. God, I don't believe this!"

Keefe studied her in silence. Because he loved her so deeply he was absorbing her upset, which was proving far greater than his own. The beautiful shining masses of her hair stood out like a halo around a face that was unnaturally pale. "I admit it's quite a story. And it doesn't end there."

"Oh, no," she moaned. "Not another sexual secret?"

"A little darker than we both supposed."

Skye sat straight, the lawyer in her coming to the fore. "Spell it out, Keefe. Keep nothing back. Though I fear you've managed to up to date."

Keefe's tone turned grim. He was starting to doubt she could handle this. "Gran believes—she has no actual proof of it, please hold fast to that, Skye—that your mother was romantically involved with my Uncle Jonty."

Skye's stoic expression changed to one of sheer astonishment. *"What?"* For all her legal training she couldn't fasten on this new development. Was it fact or fiction?

"It never occurred to me, either," he told her, head bent. "I was just a little kid when Uncle Jonty was killed. We've been looking in all the wrong places."

Skye felt like all the oxygen had rushed out of her body "Oh, my God!" she gasped in horror, putting a hand to her heart. "Why didn't we just leave this alone?" Tears stood in her beautiful blue eyes. "I *knew* you were keeping something from me, something that would drive us apart."

"Never! I won't let it," he said forcefully. "We'll meet this head on. Come here to me, Skye." He caught her to him, pushing her head back against his shoulder. "We can work this out. We can get to the bottom of things."

"Can we indeed?" She spoke as if she was relinquishing all hope. "We're first cousins. Isn't that what you and your grandmother believe?"

He tightened his arms powerfully around her, not about to ever let her go. "So what? What point is there in jumping the gun? It could be quite untrue. It's something Gran has fastened onto down the years. She has no real proof. Either way, I'll be damned if I'll let you go. The cousins bit isn't even a real issue. It's the shock. Our souls are linked."

"Of course. We're first cousins," she whispered, feeling too devastated to move.

"Even if you *are* Uncle Jonty's child and something inside me *screams* you aren't, it's legal for first cousins to marry in most countries of the world. The UK, Australia, most of the United States, Europe, the Middle—"

She cut him off, fiercely. "Don't tell me the law, Keefe. I'm a lawyer, remember?"

"Then use it to your advantage," he clipped off, more fiercely than he had intended but he was so afraid of losing her. "Use your expertise to straighten out fact from fiction, Skye. Gran is eighty years old. She's caught up in the taboos of her day. Medical geneticists have known for a long time there's no harm in first cousins marrying, no strong biological reason. Royalty did it all the time. There are far higher risks associated with inherited diseases and disorders within a family. Children can be born with very serious problems from the healthiest of parents. It's well documented."

"You don't have to convince me," she said sharply. "You'd marry me knowing I could be your first cousin?" She shut her eyes tightly as if to block him out. "Is it possible *your* Uncle Jonty's blood is beating in my veins?"

"It's possible, yes," he said flatly. "But highly improbable. I prefer to go on *my* gut feelings. I have never at any time had a feeling of overstepping any boundary."

"Boundary?" Outrage overcame her and she began to thump his chest. She wanted to make him see her pain and the devastation her father would suffer if such a thing was true. It couldn't be allowed to happen. "You *want* me, Keefe McGovern. Are you telling me want makes it all okay? After all, you *always* get what you want."

"Okay so *I* finish up the bad guy!" There was a steely glint in his eyes. "One small crack in the edifice and your lifelong love for me disappears."

"Maybe that part of my life is over," she said wildly. "Magic to mayhem! Your Uncle Jonty my father? God, no!"

"Stop it, Skye. Please stop now!" He trapped her flailing hands, holding them fiercely tight. "I know what a shock this is for you. Spare a thought for me. I've had some bad moments myself, trying to absorb it."

"So *you've* had a hard time. Imagine that! For all I know, you could have been harbouring these suspicions for some time, sus-

picions that have caused you to back off then come on strong.
The see-saw effect," she said bitterly. "I see it now. You and your
grandmother have nurtured a terror I could be Jonty's child."
Her beautiful face was a mask of pain and outrage.

"I assure you Jonty never entered my mind." He gave a
short, hard laugh. "I'm no liar. Not even you get to call me
one. So you can apologise right now."

She stared into his daunting face, seeing he, like her, was
deeply disturbed. "Okay I'm sorry, but I'm in despair. So you
don't think Uncle Jonty. That leaves Dad. No one else, is
there?" Frightened, she flashed onto something quite macabre
then she began to pull away from him, the colour completely
gone from her face. "Who else, Keefe?" She waved her hands
about in agitation. "No, that's too, too *crazy*! Could you
possibly have believed even for a split second it might have
been your *father*?"

With an oath, he swooped. "If I *did* confront such a fear,"
he confessed harshly, "I swear it hovered in my mind for just
that, a split second. My father was a great man. An hon-
ourable man. I admit I've had moments of wondering who
your biological father might be if not Jack. We all knew so
little about your mother and her past. There was no openness
as there would have been with anyone else. What was the big
mystery? We were left trying to shift around the pieces of a
puzzle. Could it have been someone out of your mother's
recent past? Someone she had fled? Never for me was it
someone with a McGovern face. Only Gran managed to
convince herself you're Jonty's child. There's no proof. Gran
jumped to conclusions. As a lawyer you know that's no way
good enough. There must be proof."

Skye's heart shrivelled. "Your grandmother is a highly intelligent woman. A mother and a grandmother. A woman with
a lot of experience of life and human nature. She must have
seen my mother and Jonty together. They must have been

together often. My mother stayed at the house. She lived with the family on and off. I've *rarely* thought about your Uncle Jonty. I wasn't even born when he died. He played no part in my life, though I knew his was a tragic story. But no more than my mother's. My *dad* has always been there for me. And he *is* my dad." She broke off in acute distress. "God knows what he'd do if he was told otherwise. I think he'd just ride off into the sunset and never be seen again. He worshipped my mother. He adores me. No. Absolutely *no*! Keefe, your *Uncle Jonty* is not my father. Jonty is *dead*."

Gently but very firmly Keefe held her, upset by the tremors that racked her body. Her suffering tore at his heart. "A DNA test would expose the truth."

She broke his strong grasp. Using the sheer force of her anger and outrage, she flew to her feet. "You think for one moment I'm going to go up to Dad and say, 'Listen there's a chance I'm not your daughter, but Jonty McGovern's'?" There was so much emotion in her voice it broke. "I wouldn't be sur-prised if he dropped down dead. I'd have to get out of your life, Keefe, before I destroyed my father's."

Here it was. His greatest fear spoken aloud. The destruc-tion of their love. "You think I'd let you do that?" He too shot to his feet, towering over her. "Do you really think I would make you so unhappy? I *love* you, Skye. We have to work this out together. No way will I let you leave me. But tell me honestly. Don't you at least want the truth?"

"Do *you*?" she lashed back. "What if your *heir*—our child—is born with some defect?"

His handsome face turned to granite. "Such a child would be accepted, loved and cared for," he said sternly. "Use your educated mind, Skye. You're not of my grandmother's gen-eration. Why do you suppose the most highly civilised coun-tries on earth allow cousin marriages? Anyway, that's not *my* thinking. You're *not* my cousin."

"Then who the hell am I?" she shouted, seriously overwound.

"You're Jack McCory's daughter."

"So why do you always call him Jack instead of referring to him as my dad?' she challenged, blazing hostility in her blue eyes.

Keefe was forced to recognise the paradox. "I've always called him Jack," he answered, knowing it sounded lame. "What else would I call him?" he fired. "Now, that's enough!" He hauled her back into his arms. "I've flown all the way to see you. To speak to you."

"You're a fiercely busy man, after all." She pushed wildly against him, feeling shame that right in the middle of it she was seized by sexual longing. She wanted him so badly she felt mortified.

"Don't turn hostile, Skye," he begged. "Either you love me or you don't. Either you'll be my wife or you won't. Are you listening?" He shook her lightly. She was all eyes with shock.

She broke off, exhausted, like a boxer pitted against far too formidable an opponent. Outclassed. Outweighed. Slowly she raised her hands in a gesture of surrender. "Oh, Keefe, what are we going to do?" This was the man who had taken her virginity. But hadn't she given it up to him as though it had been ordained? She'd had him inside her. Inside her body. Inside her heart. Inside her mind. She couldn't love another man. Not after Keefe. There would only be Keefe. Yet never in her wildest dreams had she seen Jonty McGovern as anything but a McGovern tragedy.

"The best way out of this is to get Jack's DNA," Keefe said, in a calming tone of voice. "No need to ask him. The effects, as you say, could be tragic. We test your DNA against his. He wouldn't have to know. *Ever.* We could gain, Skye, not *lose.* You're convinced Jack is your father. I'm convinced you're not my cousin. Why don't we allow our intuitions to reign?"

She thought that at any minute she might faint. "Don't secrets trash lives?" she said with great sorrow, feeling the full brunt of this last revelation. "Your grandmother felt she had a duty to me. But she couldn't bring herself to acknowledge me. I was Jack McCory the overseer's little daughter. She wasn't going to have illegitimacy darken your door. A blemish on the splendid McGovern record. McGovern money paid for my fine education. I've always been asked up to the house. But *never* acknowledged, for all her beliefs. And to think she's functioned all these years believing me to be her granddaughter."

"Oh, Skye!" he groaned. What his grandmother had done was beyond him.

She gave him the saddest smile. "The McGoverns are such snobs."

"That would be very worrying if it was true," he said shortly. "My grandmother did what she thought to be right."

"If that had have been me, I don't think I'd have been able to function at all. Turning your back on your dead son's child?" Her voice trailed off.

"Only you're *not!*" he said with far more conviction that he actually felt. "Gran is an old lady. She has lived by her lights. We have to leave it at that. No point in heaping blame on her frail shoulders. I'm sure she has suffered in her way. The irony is she got it all wrong. She would never have seen Jack as a suitor for your mother. Jonty, on the other hand, would have been. It's a class thing, as you claim."

"Don't I know it!" She heard the bitterness in her own voice. "So how do we go about this thing?"

"You could leave it to me." Tension was in his body, the slant of his taut cheekbones, the set of his chiselled mouth. "A hair from Jack's head would do it. Easy enough to get."

"Like some horrid soap opera." She held a hand to her pounding head.

"No soap opera, Skye. This is real life. We have to know the truth. Whatever it is, it changes nothing between us. Jack need know *nothing.*"

"Because there's *nothing* to know!" She whirled away.

"Don't ruin what we have." He was on her in a heartbeat. 'I love you. I need you. I want you. There *has* to be a resolution. We're living in an uncertain, unresolved present. We must look to the future. I won't let the past rule our lives."

She didn't even try to strain against the cage of his arms. Hunger for him had gained ascendancy, flooding her veins with sexual heat. She took a deep shuddering breath. "Let's face it, your power over me is too complete."

"No more than yours over me!" he countered fiercely, rapidly becoming blind to everything but his need for her. He was ravenously, painfully aroused. "Nothing and no one will take you from me and you *know* it. Let me love you. Don't struggle. Nothing else makes sense."

She leaned heavily into him, feeling deep down in her body the little jolting currents of electricity. "You win, Keefe," she said in a subdued voice. "You always win. Do what you want."

"Do we have an option?" He stared down at her with such naked desire her senses reeled. "It's this *not* knowing that is complicating our lives."

Her blue eyes were ablaze. "I love you, Keefe McGovern," she said emotionally, "but if any harm comes to my father, I swear I'll disappear from your life."

"Don't say that." He put an urgent finger to her lips. "You're in shock."

"Certainly I am." She was possessed by a sense of foreboding. "But I mean what I say. Whatever the outcome, I want your word my father is to know nothing."

"You have it. Need you ask?" He didn't want to be angry with her—she was distressed enough—but he was.

"You don't have to do anything," she said, coming to a decision. "We're talking about *my* father." Her whole demeanour had changed. "I have a case before the court. There should be a ruling mid-week. I could get a colleague to stand in for me if I had to. That way I could fly back with you. Spend the weekend with Dad. Be back in the office late Monday."

"If that's what you want. I'll arrange a charter flight to fly you back. No need then to lose time changing planes."

"Good, then that's decided." She spoke crisply, on the surface in charge of herself. What lay beneath was searing confusion.

"I didn't say it was a good plan." Keefe kept his eyes on her. "It's the *only* plan."

"Well, my heart isn't in it."

"And you think my heart is? Jack is the key to unlock the secrets of the past, Skye, not Gran."

"Yet your Uncle Jonty must have been in love with my mother," she reasoned. "At least seriously attracted to her. Your grandmother would know."

"You think I haven't considered that?" Keefe's tone was terse. "He probably was. But, God, he was just a kid. They were both a pair of kids. Maybe they were just flirting with each other. It was Jack she turned to."

"You mean she knew she had no future with Jonty." She didn't bother to hide the raw pain.

"I don't mean that at all." He shook his head, clearly upset.

Yet she persisted. "My mother was a protégée of your grandmother's. What was she doing meeting up with a station hand?"

Keefe was careful to answer. "Love will find a way. *We* know that."

"That's not really an answer."

"It's the best I can do," he said, his expression taut. "Getting Jack's DNA will provide us with an answer once and for all."

"Dad's birthday is at the end of the month. I'll say my surprise visit is an early birthday call. God, I could weep for the lie!" she said poignantly.

"It's not wrong to do this, Skye." He was losing the battle to bank down the tumult in his blood.

"So back to Djinjara. Home, sweet home! Only I've never felt like I had a real home."

"It takes a woman to make a home. *You're* the woman to make a home for me. For us. For our children. If you're not as strongly committed to your life as a lawyer as you'd once thought, you'll have an opportunity to forge another career as a photographer. I'll give you all the help you need." His hands began to move over her, every caress eloquent with desire. "In the end there's only you and me. It's always been like that. If it turns out you're my cousin, so be it! No one will stand in our way."

She let her head fall forward onto his chest. "You *want* to believe, Keefe," she said quietly. "So do I."

"Look at me."

She raised her head, her long lashes sweeping down on her cheeks. She was sick of it all. Sick of the torment. Her need for him was causing ripples to run the length of her body. Keefe's mouth descended hungrily on hers…

He was the most heart-breakingly ardent and masterful lover…

All else was silenced.

CHAPTER SEVEN

His back wedged against a tree, Scott lit up a cigarette, took a deep drag, all the while watching Jack through a veil of blue-grey smoke. They had spent all day at the toughest, most back-breaking work of all, driving the cattle out of the lignum swamps. Most of them had clean skins, not many bore the Djinjara brand. A couple of rogue bulls got clean away. They could be picked up another time. The weary stockmen were sitting about on fallen logs, talking quietly among themselves and gulping down scalding billy tea. The Chinese cook had big thick slices of freshly baked damper ready for them, smothered in either home-made jam or bush honey. Ugh! Unlike Keefe, he liked to sit apart from the men, welcoming his own company. He lifted his eyes to the blindingly blue sky. A falcon was floating above the yarding area, nearly motion-less on an upper current. Bonding with station employees had been left out of his make-up. Come to think of it, he was, by and large, a loner by nature. Either that or he wasn't into friendships. A psychological profile might even categorise him as an outsider.

Outsider or not, he had fantasised about Skye more times than he could remember. Even when he was with Jemma, it was Skye he held captive in his arms. Why were Keefe and

Skye spinning their wheels about the possibility of being first cousins? As far as he knew, it was perfectly legal for first cousins to marry. He knew quite a few second cousins within landed families who had married and raised healthy broods of kids. No, it was McCory they were worried about. How McCory would react. He knew their overseer to be physically brave. He pitched into the most difficult and dangerous of jobs. He was an excellent overseer, much admired among the nation's top cattlemen. It was his mental state that might bring McCory to his knees.

Once he knew.

Scott drew the cigarette smoke deep into his lungs. He would wait until sundown, and then follow Jack to his bungalow for a little chat. Jack would be most surprised to have him for a visitor. It had never happened before. Keefe was due to fly in before noon next day. That's if he could drag himself away from his precious Skye. At that moment Scott would have given anything to have what his brother had:

Skye McCory.

Don't do this, a warning voice started up inside his head. *Don't do it. Up until this point you haven't done anything really bad.*

That was the decent half of him talking. The McGovern half. But he knew as he continued to stare across at tall lanky Jack McCory, laughing amiably with the men, that he *was* going to do it. He had a vengeful streak, so raw and bitter it even stung him. His brother could have any woman he wanted. With Skye out of the way, the competition might have a chance. Think of it that way. It seemed incredible to him that his Uncle Jonty had mated with that other trouble-maker, Cathy-Katrina, whoever she was. But such was the power of a beautiful woman. They could turn a man into a hero or a villain. He could justify his actions on the grounds of pushing his beloved brother back from the brink. And he *did* love Keefe. It was Skye he hated. Skye who had looked at him with scorn and contempt in her eyes. No woman was allowed to do that. This was the only way he could figure out to split her and his brother up. That overheard conversation between Keefe and their grandmother had been handed to him like a gift. Gifts needed to be opened up…

Rachelle met her in the entrance hall, hostility naked in her dark eyes, her chin upthrust at an arrogant angle. "You're here to see my grandmother."

Skye nodded, studying Rachelle with a hint of pity. The sooner Rachelle made a life for herself the better. She was twenty-six years old. She had never held down a job in her entire adult life. It wasn't that she lacked intelligence, even high intelligence. Rachelle lacked any real purpose in life. Sad but true—money often robbed the inheritors of wealth of drive.

"Why are you looking at me like that?" Rachelle burst out, feeling as though she was under a microscope. If the truth be known, underneath it all she felt admiration for Skye and what she had achieved. Not that she was ever going to show it.

"Is there a correct way to look at you, Rachelle?" Skye asked mildly. "I've always wanted us to be friends but your friendship has never been on offer. Now, I'd like to see Lady Margaret. Keefe has already spoken to her. She's expecting my visit."

"You're the last person I want as a member of my family," Rachelle told her vehemently.

Skye was stopped in her tracks. Could Keefe have possibly taken his sister into his confidence? He could have only been at the homestead thirty minutes at the outside, before going off on station business. He had promised to arrange this visit with his grandmother. "So you must think something is happening?"

Rachelle didn't hesitate. "I'm not such a fool I don't know you and Keefe are joined at the hip. It's even possible you're beginning to get the upper hand. What are you seeing Gran about?"

"I see no reason not to tell you, Rachelle. I want to speak to her about my mother."

"There's been a hell of a lot of mileage in your mother's story. From all accounts she was a lady, even, would you believe, connected in some way to an aristocratic family, yet she married your father. Another shotgun affair, I suppose."

A bolt of molten anger shot through Skye, but she ignored the insult. "That's why I want to see your grandmother. There are a lot of things still unclear. Excuse me, please, Rachelle. You really need to lighten up for your own sake as much as anyone else's."

Keefe took the Land Rover, driving out of the compound, heading for Yellow Creek where some of the men would be yarding clean skins. He had briefed Jack before he had left. First on the agenda was to clear out the lignum swamps. He had every confidence in Jack to carry out his orders to the letter. He had a lot of respect for Jack. As he drove out of the trees that surrounded Yellow Creek and into the sunlit yarding paddock, his eyes skimmed the busy stockmen, looking for his overseer. No sign of him. One of the men, Whitey, a part aboriginal with a fine head of snow-white curls, was standing over by the truck, having a gash in his arm treated. Obviously Whitey had come too close to a rushing bullock's horn. Usually the shouts and calls around the yards were cheerful, but this afternoon everyone seemed a bit subdued.

"Where's Jack, Whitey?" he called, starting to feel an element of unease. He strode to the truck, fallen bark crunching under his feet. He paused to take a look at the man's arm. It was a bad gash but Whitey as usual appeared unconcerned. "Your shots are up to date?"

"Sure, boss. Jack not bin here. Not all mornin'. Jonah checked around. No one has seen 'im. Jonah checked the bungalow, thought mebbe he was sick. Not there neither."

"Where's my brother?" Keefe asked.

"Him and Bill were pushin' some cows and calves for a drink. That'd be Kooreena Waters. Bound to find 'im there."

"It's Jack I really want," said Keefe, swatting near violently at a fly. He was worried. Always a man to rely on his gut feeling, his feelings about Jack McCory and his whereabouts weren't good. It was unheard of for Jack not to be on the job. Someone must have seen him. Had he left a note at the bungalow? Had one of the nomads that moved freely across the vast station sighted him? He couldn't have simply gone away. Whatever forces were at play, confidence that all was well was starting to drain out of him.

With a single steely gesture he brought the men into a circle. "Jack is always on the job, regular as clockwork."

"Are you worried about 'im, boss?" Eddie, the leading hand, asked.

"Yes. By the look of it, so are the rest of you. Jack should be here. I want you all to spread out. We need to find him. We need to think accident. He could be hurt. He could have taken a fall from his horse. Unlikely, but something could have happened. We have to consider an encounter with a snake. Even a blasted camel in heat. Jake, you take the truck. Bill the utility. Head back towards the line of lignum swamps. Jack could be chasing up a few that got away. The rest of you, take the horses. Each man in a different direction. Report to me when you're done. We need to find Jack."

Back at the home compound, Keefe began a systematic search of the bungalow. What was he looking for, a note? Nothing in any obvious place. Skye would have seen it, although she wouldn't have been in the bungalow long. He had arranged a meeting between Skye and his grandmother the minute he'd arrived back at the house. Skye desperately needed proof of her identity. A DNA test was the only way to go. He couldn't free his mind of her saying that if any hurt came to Jack he would lose her for ever. People in shock said such things. That was his only comfort.

Skye had left the front door open. A breeze was sweeping in. Keefe went to close it. Only then did he see the grey envelope that must have flown off the hall table and headed towards the old grandfather clock, where it was stuck between the clock and the wall. For a few moments he stared at it in silence then he walked the few paces to pull the envelope out of its hiding place. It was addressed to him.

Keefe, promise me you won't come looking for me. I'm going out into the desert to think.

Jack.

Think? Blow your brains out? The note and the unsteadiness of the handwriting was a sure sign Jack was a very disturbed man. What had happened and very recently? He trusted his grandmother absolutely not to summon Jack for a talk. Other than his grandmother and himself, no one else knew of the conclusions they had reached. Jack would be back. He had to believe that. On the other hand, he had no intention of following Jack's request. He would have the whole station out looking for him. He would alert the nomadic aborigines. They saw everything in their travels. Even in the *mind's* eye. He would take up the chopper. He just knew he wasn't overreacting.

God, he would have to tell Skye. He checked to see if Jack had taken his rifle.

He had.

Both women stared at Keefe in shocked silence. Lady McGovern was the first to speak. "What *is* it, dear?" He cut a powerful, very daunting figure.

"I don't exactly know." He frowned. "Not yet. We can't find Jack. He could have had an accident."

Skye sprang to her feet, instantly in a panic. "Have you checked everywhere? Spoken to the men?"

"Need you ask?" He took hold of her arm to steady her. "You'll want to join the search, I know. So follow me. Don't worry, Gran." He turned back to the frail old lady. "We'll find him." It was spoken like a foregone conclusion.

But dead or alive?

They came on Rachelle tiptoeing down the stairs. "What the devil are you doing?" Keefe called to her, swiftly closing in with Skye in his wake.

"Something is going on, isn't it?" Rachelle looked from one to the other. Both looked extremely tense. A dead give-away.

Keefe stared at his sister, his black brows knotted. Rachelle as a child had always been a great one for hiding behind doors, curtains, sofas anywhere she could overhear private conversations. Could she possibly have been outside their grandmother's bedroom door the night when they had been having their very private conversation? It didn't seem likely. Rachelle had been deeply involved in the card game when he had left the room.

"My father is missing, Rachelle," Skye burst out raggedly, wanting to push Rachelle out of the way. She didn't trust her at all. "Keefe has sent out a search party. Would you know anything about his disappearance?' She did something awful then. She seized Rachelle's arm in a painful grip.

"Me?" Rachelle pulled away in shock. "What do you take me for? I have no idea what the men are doing! Not interested either. He could have taken a fall from his horse. Happens all the time. Horses are dreadfully unpredictable creatures, especially when they're spooked."

"You *know*, don't you?" Driven by worry, Skye, the taller, went to shake her. "Tell us what you know."

"Are you mad? Let go of me!" Rachelle struggled wildly but Skye held on. "Keefe, make her let go of me."

Keefe took Skye away, holding her firmly by his side. "We need you to answer one simple question, Rachelle. The truth, please. Have you spoken to Jack McCory in the last couple of days?"

"Jack McCory's a friend of mine?" Rachelle asked acidly, raising her brows heavenwards. "How dare you lay hands on me, Skye McCory. I have no idea what the two of you are getting at."

"Well, I'll tell you," Keefe rasped. "For a lot of your life you've made a habit of eavesdropping, Rachelle."

"It's not a crime, is it?" Rachelle flushed violently with embarrassment.

"When the Templetons were here and you were enjoying yourselves playing cards, I went upstairs to talk to Gran. Did you follow me?"

"Follow you?" Rachelle asked cautiously, eyeing first her brother then Skye.

"Answer the question." Skye's voice rose sharply. "Did you overhear what Keefe and your grandmother were saying?"

Rachelle's face visibly paled. "I may have been guilty of eavesdropping in the past. In this family it's the only way you find out anything. But I swear I didn't follow you upstairs. Ask anyone."

"They've all gone home."

"Scott hasn't. Ask him."

A shudder passed through Skye. "Did Scott go upstairs? Did he leave the room?"

Rachelle fought the impulse to cry. It wasn't something she normally did, but the upset was contagious. "I'm sure he didn't. He watched when he didn't play."

"You're certain of that?" Keefe questioned. "I mean, you get engrossed in the game. I've seen you too many times."

"Why don't you tell me what's going on?" Rachelle to her horror felt a tear trickle down her cheek. "Everyone hates me."

"Rubbish! You go out of your way to be unpleasant. You've

done your best to upset Skye over the years. But no one hates you, Rachelle. I love you. Be assured of that. I just live in hope you'll get yourself together. So we can take it you didn't speak to Jack."

"Definitely not!" Rachelle's dark eyes flashed. "What could I possibly say to him anyway? What could it be that would make Jack McCory disappear?" Slowly she turned to focus on Skye, lifting her hands in a gesture of supplication. "I swear to you, Skye, I would do nothing to upset your father. I've just lost my own father. I think about him all the time. Whatever has happened, I could play no part in your father's disappearance. I beg you to believe me."

Skye remained staring into Rachelle's brimming eyes. At last she said, "I do believe you, Rachelle. I'm very sorry if we've upset you. We're tremendously worried about Dad."

"You can't find him anywhere?" Relieved, Rachelle dashed her tears away with the back of her hand.

"I'm afraid not."

"So there are places I can search," Rachelle offered.

"Thank you for that." Skye started to turn away, her mind crowded with fears for her father's safety.

"The best thing you can do, Rachelle, is go keep Gran company," Keefe said. "She's as distressed as the rest of us. I'm taking the chopper up. I'm confident we'll find Jack in the desert. But I need to conduct the search before nightfall."

"All the luck in the world!" Rachelle called, feeling chastened.

When they were gone, she lowered her head for a moment, biting her lip and thinking back hard… *Had* Scott been there all the time? She wasn't one hundred per cent sure. What *was* it Keefe and Gran had been discussing? Whatever it was, it had a bearing on Jack McCory's disappearance. Rachelle began to murmur a little prayer for his safety.

Please, God, please protect Jack McCory.

* * *

They had two hours before darkness. The men on the ground had searched steadily without finding any trace of the overseer. He let the search go on even though Jack had written he was heading into the desert. He could have been laying down a false trail.

From the air they looked down on an infinite landscape of savage splendour without sign of human habitation. A man in a moving vehicle would be easily exposed in this trackless wilderness. Without a good supply of water, that man could easily die. Many had lost their lives in the country's vast interior; great deserts covered almost half the continent. Fiery red sand dunes rose up from the plains, peaking and curling like the waves of the inland sea of pre-history. Between the giant swells the troughs were clothed in the ubiquitous spinifex and thick clumps of hardy grasses, stunted trees of mulga and mallee. There was very little protection from a blazing sun out here. On the gibber plains in the distance, the large boulders, rocks, stones and pebbles glittered like some incredible mosaic. Above them the mirage shimmered in silvery glass whirlpools.

It was in its way fantastically beautiful—especially to Skye with her photographer's eye—only she had no mind to admire it. Her father could be dead or dying down there.

Eyes peeled, they scoured the vast empty expanses, with their dried-up red clay pans and ancient watercourses that appeared like white veins amid the red. They had been flying for approximately thirty minutes when Skye, who had her head turned in the opposite direction to Keefe, tapped him urgently on the shoulder.

"Down there. Could that be the station Jeep?"

"If it is, Jack has used dead branches and bleached grasses to screen it from view." Immediately Keefe brought the chopper down low… They weren't all that far off being earth-bound. Both of them had picked up the image of a vehicle now.

Feet from landing, the downdraft of the rotor flattened the

tall spears of the spinifex grass and churned up a mini-dust-storm. Skye struggled to free herself from her seat. She was so agitated Keefe had to take over. "Try to keep calm, Skye," he told her. "We need to keep calm, okay?"

"I'll try." She was having difficulty just swallowing. Her heart seemed to be occupying her entire mouth How much of a lie was her life? It didn't seem to matter now. All that mattered was finding the man she called her father alive. Nothing could destroy the love they had for each other. She was desperate to tell him. How many bereaved families had missed just such a chance to tell their loved ones how greatly they were loved and needed?

Feet dug into the desert sand, with the red whirlpool slowly abating, Keefe lowered a hand to her shoulder. "I want you to wait here." He spoke with habitual authority. "Promise me you'll do that. Wait until I give the signal. You have to trust me, Skye, to know what's best."

"You think he's killed himself, don't you?" She could hear the panic and grief in her voice.

"I think Jack's got more guts than that," Keefe clipped off. "Maybe he's just plain drunk and sleeping it off. Give me a minute and I'll find out."

It was the longest minute of her life.

I'll do anything, God. I'll give up Keefe, the man I love with all my heart, if I have to. I'll tear out my own heart. Don't do this to me, Dad!

What she was offering was self-sacrifice.

Keefe stepped out of the makeshift shelter, waving his arm in an all-clear. "Right, Skye," he yelled. "You can come now."

Gasping for breath, the heat scorching her neck, she covered the distance as quickly as she had covered any distance in her life, powered by sheer desperation to check on her father's condition. The loose sand and the unforgiving heat coming off it was making the going tough, but she was tougher. As she reached Keefe, she half stumbled and he caught her up, hauling her into his arms. "Stop tearing yourself to pieces, Skye. I can't bear it. Jack's in a bit of a mess, but he's going to be all right."

It was moderate rather than severe dehydration Keefe had diagnosed quite accurately, though that situation could have swiftly changed. It didn't take long for even a physically fit man to succumb to killer dehydration in the desert. Especially a man who had polished off a bottle of whisky.

With her head bent low to clear the overhang of branches, Skye entered the shelter. Her father was sitting on the sand, a man at rock bottom. His head and his torso were soaked from the contents of a canvas water bottle Keefe had poured over him. Unlike her, Keefe had had the presence of mind to take it out of the chopper and bring it with him.

"Dad?" Realising she was shouting with relief and gratitude, Skye reined herself in. "Dad, Dad!" Love shone from her face and her voice. "What an awful fright you gave us. Don't you dare ever do it again. Don't you *dare*. You hear me?"

Jack, conscious but weak and dehydrated, somehow managed a smile. "What are you doing here, love?" His look of desolation was pitiful, yet his blue eyes flickered with sudden light.

"Where else would I be?" Skye felt the tears roll down her cheeks. The sight of her father so reduced, plus the reek of alcohol, was almost more than she could bear. She threw herself down alongside him, swooped on him, gathering him close and raining kisses on his cheek covered with harsh stubble. "We've found you. Now we're going to take you home. It's all right, Dad. Everything is going to be all right."

"I'll go get the other water-bottle," Keefe said, getting up off his haunches to make the return trip to the chopper. He turned away, hiding a face white with fury.

He *knew* now what had happened. He just *knew* who had gone to Jack to fill his ears with black bile. He aimed to take action. Even so, payback time never felt so bad.

CHAPTER EIGHT

BACK on Djinjara it wasn't easy to get Jack to take to his bed. But it was heartening to see that slow, increased water intake, plus a cooling shower, had brought about a positive result.

"That's an order, Jack," Keefe told him firmly, long used to men obeying him. "Stay in bed. I've called in Joe McPherson to check you out, just to be on the safe side. You're BP is a bit low. Probably your body will need days for the cells to plump up again. But you're looking better."

"Do as Keefe tells you, Dad," Skye urged, taking her father's hand to offer comfort.

"Unless I'm *not* your dad," Jack murmured, in a very distressed voice.

Skye's blue eyes flashed up at Keefe, then back to her father "What are you saying?" she quavered.

"You *know*, sweetheart." He stared at the white sheet that covered him, not her.

"I know nothing of the kind." Skye stoutly maintained the lie. It was *white*, wasn't it? Well, she wasn't a saint.

"But you *want* to know?"

Skye's helpless shrug signalled her defeat. Another long look passed between herself and Keefe, who was standing on the opposite side of her father's narrow bed.

"Tell us what you *think* you know, Jack." Keefe drew up a chair, speaking quietly, persuasively to his overseer.

"I know precious little," Jack admitted with a tortured smile. "God knows, I never did ask questions. I adored Cathy, Katrina, whatever her real name. I loved her. I know I'm just an ordinary bloke, but I was sure she loved me. She told me I was the loveliest, kindest man in the world." His voice broke.

"Of course she loved you," Skye maintained hotly, taking her father's hand. "And so you are a lovely kind man. Who told you all this, Dad?" She was convinced it was Rachelle, who had appeared genuinely upset by her father's disappearance, but that alone didn't ensure Rachelle was innocent. She was such a devious person.

"It wasn't Rachelle." Keefe looked across at her, reading her mind. This was no time to push Jack.

Skye was aware he was giving off signals. But she felt compelled to ignore them. She had to get to the bottom of this. "Was it Scott?" Scott, who had long desired her, now hated her. It had to be Scott. That was his nature.

Keefe spoke gently. "Will you confirm that, Jack?"

Jack subsided miserably into the pillows. "Leave it for a little while, will you, Keefe?" he quietly begged. "I feel a bit under the weather at the moment."

"Of course." Keefe pushed back his chair and stood up resolutely. "It doesn't matter anyway, Jack. I know it was my brother." His handsome face was set like granite. "Rest easy, Jack. I'll take care of this. McPherson will be here shortly to take a look at you. When you're feeling better we'll arrange a short holiday for you. Be assured, your job is as safe as ever."

As Keefe strode from the room, Skye hurried after him, reaching out to grasp his arm in an effort to detain him. "What are you going to do, Keefe?"

He turned back, studying her beautiful, agonised face. "Leave it to me, Skye," he said, not about to accept interference, even from her. "We both know it *was* Scott. He meant to hurt you through your father. He didn't give a damn what happened to Jack. Jack will confirm it in his own good time."

"Yes." She sighed with deep regret. "Scott's aim has always been to destroy what we have."

"Except revenge is a double-edged sword. Now the sword is going to fall on him."

Keefe turned away. She felt compelled to run after him. He looked so angry, so menacing and he was a very strong man. Superbly fit. Scott would be no match for him. "He's your brother, Keefe." She gripped his arm, feeling the anger and bitter disillusionment that raged through him. "Tell me what you're going to do. If you love me, you'll tell me."

"*If* I love you?" He caught her up so powerfully she was momentarily off her feet. His brilliant eyes slashed incredulously over her face. "How can you even *say* it?"

She was shaking right through her body. "I'm frightened, that's why. Please tell me, Keefe. I couldn't bear for *you* to get injured. Scott wouldn't play fair. He can't seem to help himself."

"I told you to leave it to me," he repeated harshly. "Believe me, he won't stand a chance. Then I'm going to banish him. Next, I'm going to order Rachelle to find herself a job. Any job, just so long as she gets up off her pampered backside."

Skye strangled a laugh. "Wouldn't that be something?"

"This could have ended very badly, Skye. You know that."

"Dad would never have taken his own life." She had to convince herself of that. "He just wanted time to think."

"Only time was running out." Keefe's retort was grim.

She stared up into his darkly disturbed face. "We're no further than we were before. I can't possibly ask dad for a DNA sample. Not now."

"The plan goes ahead." He bent to press a hard kiss onto her mouth. It burned like a brand. Just as he had intended.

"If you can be patient, you'll find Jack is prepared to give it. He's a good man. Doing what *you* need is part of Jack's goodness. I'd strongly advise you to let him bring up the subject himself. Now, don't try to detain me. I'm going in search of my brother." He released her so quickly she staggered a little. "There's absolutely *nowhere* Scott can hide. Nowhere I can't find him."

Dr Joe McPherson of the Royal Flying Doctor Service flew in an hour later, and carefully checked Jack over. No questions were asked apart from those about Jack's symptoms. Dr McPherson handed Skye a list of things to do to help her father recover quickly. Hospitalisation wasn't called for. Maybe a bit of counselling later. No reference was made as to what the counselling might be for, but obviously Joe McPherson knew. He tended to know everything about the people in his vast practice.

Afterwards Jack slept. When he awoke it was to find Skye by his bedside, quietly reading a book of poetry. "Feeling better, Dad?" She closed the book—she hadn't been taking all that much in—setting it down on the bedside table. "Anything I can get you? A cup of tea?"

"Tea would be lovely," he said. "My throat is so dry."

In a matter of minutes Skye was back, allowing her father to sip the tea in silence before taking the empty cup from him.

"That was good," Jack sighed, allowing her to plump up the pillows. "It's dark.'

"Eight o'clock, Dad."

"Has Keefe come in again?" Urgency was in his hoarsened voice.

"Not as yet." She shook her head. "But he will. You don't have to talk, Dad, if you don't want to. Not *ever*!"

"Only it's my plain duty to talk," he said with a wry grimace. "I don't know *what* I intended to do, darling girl, out there in the desert. I was temporarily off my head. But the desert makes a man feel as small and unimportant in the scheme of things as a grain of sand. My excuse is I was in a terrible state of shock."

"I know that, Dad." Skye covered one rough calloused hand with her own.

"I didn't deserve Cathy," Jack said. "I don't deserve you."

Skye held back tears. "Now you're being way too modest." She smiled.

"Maybe just plain stupid," Jack answered brusquely. "Just a naïve old cowhand. You want to know for sure, don't you?"

Skye held his blue eyes. "I'm sure you're my dad. That's all that matters." She pressed his hand tightly.

"I don't think so." Jack's answer was uncharacteristically grim. "You love Keefe?"

"With all my heart. Minus the part you've got." She tried for another smile. "We want to marry, Dad. Keefe is insistent. But I can't see to a future with a cloud hanging over our heads. First, we get *you* right. I couldn't have borne to lose you, Dad. Remember that when you're feeling low. Behind you, there's *me*. Never forget you have to answer to *me*."

"That's my girl!" For the first time Jack gave a big open smile. "I knew Cathy had a bit of a crush on Jonty," he revealed, gently scratching his chest. "God, he was handsome and so full of life. A McGovern. Only Jonty was more or less spoken for. He was involved with one of the Corbett girls. Louise, as I recall. A pretty girl, a very suitable young lady, but not a patch on your mother, who was a genuine beauty. As you are. I was sure Cathy understood that."

"So it was accepted that Jonty McGovern and Louise Corbett belonged together?"

"That was the word. At any rate, Louise had a nervous breakdown after Jonty was killed. He always was a bit of a daredevil, taking unnecessary risks, yet a tragic accident all the same. Cathy, too, was tremendously upset. Everyone was. Jonty was so young to be taken like that."

Skye gave his cheek an encouraging stroke. "How did you get to know my mother so well?"

"Like I've always told you, sweetheart. For me it was love at first sight. How it happened was like this, something of a miracle for me, I can tell you. Lady McGovern charged me of all people to take Cathy out on trips around the station. I was always considered to be very trustworthy and responsible. Personally I always believed she sent me out with Cathy so Cathy couldn't be with Jonty."

"That could certainly have been true," Skye said, with a lick of bitterness. She still hadn't forgiven Lady McGovern. Perhaps she never would. "So on these trips you got to know one another very well?"

"Darned right!" Jack replied with conviction. "We hit it off from the beginning. I want you to know I behaved like a true gentleman all the time. Dozens of times I wanted to kiss her. The urge got more and more powerful every time we were together. But I never laid a finger on my Cathy except to assist her in some way. Getting in and out of vehicles. Dismounting. That sort of thing. In a short space of time we became really good mates. I was always skilful in the bush, a good bushman. I've always been close to the aboriginal people. They showed me lots. I, in turn, showed Cathy lots. She loved this place. She never wanted to leave. She didn't talk about her past. I accepted her background must have been painful. I never pried. She would tell me when she was good and ready, I reckoned. Only I lost her. Maybe I was *meant* to lose her," he said in one of the saddest voices Skye had ever heard.

"Don't say that, Dad." She let her head rest against his, listening to him draw in a ragged breath.

"There are jealous gods up there, Skye. Believe it. One

shouldn't love anyone too much. Love and loss go hand in hand. If you lose the person you love, your heart is ripped from your body."

"I believe that." She spoke from the depths of her deep, passionate and abiding love for Keefe.

"Now, let's see about this DNA test," Jack said briskly, as though they had been discussing it all along.

"Not necessary, Dad." She looked him directly in the eyes. She was aware of the DNA profiles for close relationships such as first cousins. She was also aware that the results were inconclusive. It was her father's DNA that was needed.

"We'll do it!" he said firmly. "I'm certain in my heart you're *my* child, Skye. I refuse to dishonour your mother and her memory. Cathy would never have done that to me. At first I was shocked out of my mind by what Scott told me. He has such a dark streak. But I've been over and over it out there in the desert. She wouldn't have done it. That wasn't my girl, my Cathy. If it was Jonty McGovern's child she carried, she would have told me. She knew I would have helped her in any way I could. I would have been shocked but, God, I loved her. I saw myself as her protector."

"I believe you about everything, Dad" Skye tried to fill up the raw aching spots in her with trust.

"And I believed in Cathy," Jack said. "Lady McGovern got it all wrong. The thing is, love, and you have to take it into account, she never for one moment considered me as a likely suitor for Cathy. God forbid! Cathy was a lady. Say what you like, the old lady is a snob. Can't help it, you see. To her I simply didn't count. It *had* to be Jonty. Jonty was the father of Cathy's child. Let's prove it to her once and for all that she was wrong."

Keefe called at the bungalow an hour later.

"How's Jack now?" Voice pitched low, he walked into the

comfortable living room, his height and physical magnificence making the adequate space seem claustrophobically small.

"Sleeping peacefully," she said, picking up on his deep distress. "You spoke to Scott?"

Keefe nodded, putting out his arm and drawing her to him. "Among other things," he said bluntly. "He's up at the house now. Packing. He'll go to wherever I send him. It was going to be Moolaki. It's now Emerald Waters in the Gulf. He'll be up close and personal with the crocs."

"Oh, Lord! How did he take it?" Skye stared up at his taut face, seeing the underlying distress.

"He was absolutely *delighted*. What else?"

"You're upset."

"Of course I'm upset!" His silver eyes flashed. "Scott is my brother. He can fill me with a black rage—he's such a liar—full of bitterness and resentment. He has always wanted to be me, even though he has no real insight into what that entails. He's a terrible disappointment, but he's still my brother."

"I understand that, Keefe." She did. "I know you're suffering. But I need to know this. Are you blaming me in some way?"

"Good God, what are you talking about?" He stared down at her with a knotted frown.

She broke away, going to the door that shut the living room off from the hallway and closing it. "Remember years ago when Scott came after me?" she questioned, a searching look in her eyes.

He cut her off at once. "I'll never forget it."

Something in his manner set off a perverse spark of anger. It had been an extremely stressful day. Both of them were nearing the end of their tethers yet—or perhaps because of it—she couldn't stop. "You may deny it now, Keefe, but you practically accused me *then* of being the catalyst in the whole episode. I was the innocent victim yet didn't you say at the time that Scott wasn't such a monster. Remember?" she challenged. "What was I again? *Temptation on legs*, according to Scott. You appeared to agree. I've had a lot of trouble with that one," she said.

Keefe stood there, disgusted by the havoc Scott had wreaked on them. He could see the tension and the hurt—the remembered and the present—in every line of her body.

"I hurt you," he acknowledged. "I didn't mean to. But it was so *difficult* then. I was sick with concern about you, disgusted with Scott, but, forgive me, I saw you in the heat of the moment as what he said. Temptation. From a little girl you had turned into the most beautiful, alluring woman right before our eyes. Even level-headed men can become a little crazy around a woman like that."

"Like *me*, you mean?" She hugged herself, her arms wrapped around her body like a shield. "I don't see *you* acting crazy!" Her eyes were huge with delayed shock. "I don't see you acting powerless. You're the all-conquering male. You're Keefe McGovern, the cattle baron. Admired and respected by all. You could have any woman you want."

"I believe I've answered all that," Keefe's expression was that of a man nearing the end of his tether. "Over and over. *You're* the only woman I want. *You're* the only woman I'll ever want. Stop now, Skye. It's been one hell of a day. We'll talk in the morning. Thank God Jack is safe." He turned to move away, but she couldn't let him go without *touching* him, feeding off his strength. Whatever the frustrations, whatever the difficulties, she could never be deprived of the sight and sound of Keefe.

"I'm sorry. Forgive me," she whispered, putting her hand on his shoulder and staring up into the dark intensity in his face.

"Nothing to be sorry for," he muttered, pulling her to him and taking her mouth. "Come riding with me in the morning." His arms wound powerfully, protectively around her. "At dawn, just the two of us. You being here and me at the House is much too cruel. I need to make love to you, hold you through the night." His breath rasped in his chest. His body was tuned to such a pitch he didn't think he could take any more of these frustrations. Time after time. He wanted to close the door on the lot of them. Erect a huge barrier between Skye and himself and the demands of the outside world. Jack just had to be Skye's biological father. Their whole future appeared to ride on it. Skye was a woman of strong passions. Strong convictions.

"I need to wake up beside you," she murmured back. She had thought in her brightest moments that their being together was pre-destined, now she was constantly reminded of the promise she had made to a God who had shown her mercy. She had her father back.

It was probably the most dramatic entrance Rachelle would ever make in her life. She charged up the short flight of front steps and onto the porch, crying out Keefe's name. In the next instant she crashed into the living room, her face ghostly white. "You've got to come," she gasped, bending over to hold a hand to the stitch in her side. "Scott is going off his rocker. He's shouting at Gran. It's going to give her a heart attack if he keeps it up. He's accusing her of loving you more than all of us put together. He said you're sending him away to be eaten by the crocs. I hope they get him," she cried with savage gusto. "He said you hate him and it's all Skye's fault. That she's our *cousin*. Our *first* cousin, Uncle Jonty's child. Is that true?" Rachelle's dark eyes were nearly starting out of her head.

"No, it's not!" Keefe wasn't going to be caught up in specu-lation. For a start, even he wasn't certain. He went to his sister's side, enfolding her shaking body in his arms. "Quiet now, Chelle. Hush. Get your breath back. I'm on my way."

"I'll come with you," Skye said, in no mood to brook an objection. How could Scott do this to his eighty-year-old-grandmother? Lady McGovern's health since the death of her son, Broderick, had markedly declined.

"Me, too." Rachelle sobered, enormously gratified by the comfort she had found in her brother. "Will your dad be okay?" She looked at Skye, who nodded.

"Dad's asleep. It's the sleep of exhaustion."

"We're all glad he's back where he belongs, Skye. I mean, I haven't been much of a friend to you."

"But you can be a tremendous help in the future." Skye had no difficulty offering an olive branch.

Keefe drove the Jeep to the base of the homestead's stone steps. He sprang out of the vehicle with the uncoiled strength and liquid grace of a jungle cat. And, it had to be said, something of their ferocity too. The two young women followed him more slowly, Rachelle for the first time in her life clinging to Skye's hand.

"I can't believe Scott could turn on Gran like this," she wailed. "He's always been volatile. This time he's blown a fuse."

"Where are they, Chelle?" Keefe called from over his shoulder.

"Gran's bedroom. Keefe must have hurt him," she confided to Skye in an aside. "His face is a bit of a mess."

"Keefe wouldn't have hurt him too much." Skye hoped. "He knows his own strength. He wouldn't turn the full force of it on his brother."

"Scott well deserves it," Rachelle said, appalled by her brother's behaviour. "Gran is absolutely off limits. He nearly scared me to death. Gran wasn't showing any of it. She's tough. But she's old now. Scott really does have a vicious streak."

The two of them followed Keefe up the grand staircase at a rush, but he had already disappeared down the corridor. The house was silent. Yet neither young woman found this calming. "If he's caused Gran any harm I'll never forgive him," Rachelle said dazedly. "I'm so glad you're here with me, Skye. I can't possibly keep going the way I am."

They found Lady McGovern with her two grandsons in the bedroom. Rachelle went immediately to her grandmother, kneeling at her feet. "You okay, Gran?" She searched the distinguished old lady's face.

"I'm fine, dear," Lady McGovern said, though she looked far from fine. She looked old and frail. "A bit flustered, that's all. It would take more than Scott's inexcusable abuse to carry me off."

Skye, undergoing a delayed shock reaction, was suddenly hit by a dizzy spasm. She slumped back against an antique chest, nearly toppling the exquisite Chinese vase that sat on it.

"Skye?" Keefe crossed to her, guiding her into one of the armchairs. "Put your head down for a moment." He eased her golden blonde head forward, keeping his hand on her nape.

"I'm okay." She brought her head up after several seconds.

"You bet she's okay." Scott, who had been sitting with his head in his hands, suddenly came back to life. "Like we actually *need* her in the family."

"You're unstoppable, aren't you?" Lady McGovern lamented. "You need professional help.'

Scott flinched, his eyes locking on his grandmother's. "I can't believe you said that, Gran. I would never hurt you. I just wanted you to see things *my* way."

"Don't even try to justify *your* way," Keefe told his brother coldly. "Gran's right. You need counselling. After that, you can take over at Emerald Waters. If you don't want to, fine. You and Rachelle have a very healthy trust fund. You can do as you like. The problem is, Scott, you don't appear to have any real insight into your own behaviour. It's deplorable. With the right help maybe you'll be able to straighten yourself out."

"How can I begin to walk straight?" Scott gave an agonised laugh. "I've had to walk in *your* shadow for twenty-six years."

He spoke as though he perceived that to be the sole cause of his troubles. "I had no choice in the matter. I was the second son. I was *unwanted*. Wouldn't surprise me."

Lady McGovern looked sadly at her younger grandson. "You were very much wanted, Scott. Wanted and loved. What's going on here is some lack, some liability, in yourself. You're eaten up with jealousy and resentment. You're a mess, my boy. And that mess has to be cleaned up."

Scott swung his angry accusing glance Skye's way. "What about the mess *she's* made? You said yourself you thought she was Uncle Jonty's kid. There's always been a dark underbelly in this family. Skye sure doesn't look like Jack McCory."

"Jack McCory is a good man." Lady McGovern held up her hand as Keefe went to sharply intervene. "The sad thing is I've gone for far too many years not fully appreciating what sort of man he is. Cathy loved him. She tried to tell me that, but I couldn't *see* it. I thought she was infatuated with Jonty. I was blind to what was right under my nose. Jack McCory has proved himself to be a man of integrity. It was a terrible thing you did, Scott, presenting Jack with what could possibly be ill-founded assumptions. I may not be able to forgive myself for that."

"It's fact!" Scott sneered, a nerve twitching in his cheek. "The thing is, what are we going to do about it?"

"No *we*." Keefe's tone lashed. "None of this is your concern, Scott." He rested his hands on Skye's shoulders. "Skye and I are to be married."

Please, God, yes, yes, Skye silently begged. She couldn't continue without hope.

Scott's chin quivered with rage. "It'll be over in a matter of months. It's a natural reaction not to want to marry your first cousin."

"Oh, shut up, Scott," Rachelle raged. "For once in your life mind your own business. You're just jealous. I always knew you fancied Skye. But I'm ready to back whatever Keefe and Skye choose to do. First cousins can marry. No problem. Annette Kingsley—I went to school with her—married her first cousin, Brett. They have a couple of lovely kids now. You've allowed yourself to be eaten up with jealousy and envy. We've all had to live with it. You'll be better off away from here. So will I. All these years you've been trying to live Keefe's life. Time to get one of your own. I plan to."

"I want you off Djinjara tomorrow, Scott," Keefe said. "When you can return is entirely up to you."

Scott stood up, lurching to the door. "Stick your offer of Emerald Downs," he said. "I've got money. No one wants me here anyway, so I reckon I might travel. Become a playboy or a beach bum. I just can't hack marrying poor old Jemma."

"You'll be doing her a big favour," Keefe said in a deeply ironic voice.

"But Skye now!" Scott's dark eyes glowed hotly. "You mean to have Skye McCory?"

"I've already said so." Keefe didn't spare his brother his contempt.

"I won't be expecting an invitation to the wedding, then?" Scott gave Keefe then Skye an insolent salute.

"Right on!" Keefe followed his brother up, determined on seeing him to his room. "Move it, Scott. You need to pack."

CHAPTER NINE

SKYE stayed inside with her father all morning. Scott was due to fly out at noon. Events had been tough on everyone. The family was upset. So was she. It was terrible to be thought of as "the enemy", which was obviously the way Scott felt about her. She wasn't such a fool she didn't know behind the intense dislike lay a very different emotion, equally unwelcome. Scott was just as much attracted to her as he had ever been. It was part of his condition—sibling rivalry carried to the nth degree—to hunger for what his older brother had. It had started in Scott's boyhood. It had carried through to Scott the man. She knew there were areas of grief and a kind of defeat in Keefe in relation to his brother. Keefe had tried endlessly to help Scott. It hadn't worked because Scott wouldn't allow it to work. That would take away his *raison d'être*. She worried that perhaps part of Keefe was subconsciously shifting some of the blame onto her. She had seen it before, but she wouldn't tolerate it now. Keefe loved his brother for all his aberrations. That was what family was about.

She had given her father an edited version of what had happened the previous night, telling him the family had agreed Scott needed professional help to enable him to overcome his problems.

"He'll carry them to his dying day, poor lad," Jack said, his expression saddened. "Hate to say it but a lot of families have the odd man out. So what about young Jemma? Is she still in the equation?"

Skye shook her head. "For a time Jemma will suffer. She does love him. Why I don't know. I've never heard him offer her an affectionate word. There's no explaining this love business. The choices we make, even if they don't fit our needs."

"No explaining life," Jack said with a wry laugh. He was looking so much better, recovering well. "So what did the old lady say? Never darken my door again?"

"Nothing like that, Dad." Skye refilled their coffee cups. "Scott's family love him. The tragedy is he doesn't recognise it."

Jack nodded. "It's as you say. We all make choices in life. Some choices lead to great happiness, others to suffering. The trouble is we don't know at the time. Now, when do we get this test done? The sooner the better, I guess, though I'm at peace in my mind."

The implications were so strong, so possibly traumatic that Skye had deliberately blocked her mind to any other result than that Jack was her biological father. "I've been thinking about that. In the course of my work I've dealt with DNA testing on behalf of clients. All of them paternity tests, as it happens. One involved a large inheritance, only my client's late father *wasn't* her biological father."

"So she missed out?"

"On half of it. I managed to convince the rest of the family she had a definite entitlement and we would fight for it. The case was settled out of court. My client received roughly one quarter. They were a greedy lot. It wasn't the money, it was the not belonging that broke my client's heart. As far as the tests go, it takes about three or four days from the time a sample is received at the laboratory. Keefe wants you to have some time off. Why don't you come back with me? You love Sydney. We can do lots of things together."

"And it would make things easier for this testing?"

She nodded. "We're both on hand. It's Lady McGovern that has to be convinced. She's lived all these years with pure supposition. It's worn her down. Time to set her free."

"But I'm your dad no matter…right?" There was a humble note in Jack's voice.

"You bet you are!" Skye lightly punched his arm. "That's the way it is. That's the way it's always going to be. You're my dad."

She had arranged to meet Keefe mid-afternoon. Same old meeting place. They were desperate to be alone. There was so much to discuss. And above and beyond that, she craved the physical closeness. How could she bring herself to renounce Keefe? How *could* she? That was her torment, adding a great urgency to her prayers. Was it possible to bargain with God, she thought, then forget all about one's promise when the drama was over? Much as she brooded on it, she couldn't think so. It hadn't been a light promise. It had been a solemn vow. Scott had committed a crime, going to her father with his revenge-filled revelations. Now Scott had flown away, leaving the consequences of his actions behind.

She took her favourite mare, Zemira, from the stables. Zemira had that little bit of a devil in her. They forded the numerous water channels that criss-crossed the station. With some she underestimated the depth of the channel at the centre. The water came up to her knee pads, but she would dry off soon enough. The heat of the day was still intense. In the distance she could see a mob of cattle, a thousand or so, being turned in a huge wave towards water. No life without water. A great bull called Samson led the mob by several yards, his dominance on display. Heifers came respectfully behind. The lowing and bellowing—mothers for their calves—even at a distance, rent the air.

On the plain, the landscape was painted in bold colours, rust red with great splashes of dark gold from the spinifex and multiple shades of green and grey-green from the native grasses. Some of the tall grasses were flushed along the tops with tiny yellow wildflowers, bright as coins in the sun. As always, the mirage was abroad. From a distance it took the form of a silver sea, deep enough to swim in. The early explorers had headed off towards those silver seas only to tread never-ending fiery red sands.

The peace and quiet of the hill country was remarkable. Silence *could* speak. It spoke to her. Silence brought her a much-needed measure of peace. Skye attended first to the mare then she spread out a rug in the sun-dappled shade of the bauhinias. Native passion fruit were growing nearby. The pungent fragrance she inhaled with pleasure, drawing it deep into her lungs. With her pocket knife she split a couple of fruit, putting each half to her mouth and letting the pulp slide sweetly tart and thirst quenching in a cool stream down her throat. Delicious! She settled herself on the rug, looking out on the vast panorama.

What to a city person was a trackless, untamed wilderness of flaring red soil, blazing blue skies and the beautiful, but treacherous mirage held for her all the magic of the Dreamtime. This giant desert landscape was deep under her skin. She thought it would take more than a lifetime to photograph it in all its moods. Inevitably her thoughts turned to the coming of the wildflowers. No city person could imagine what it was like, riding through an ocean of wildflowers that ran on mile after mile after mile, away to the horizon. She wanted to capture that sight on camera. That time would come. All that was needed was a cyclone, even heavy monsoon rains in the tropical north. The great inland river system would fill and overflow, preceding one of the most brilliant spectacles one could witness in a lifetime.

After ten minutes of waiting she climbed to the top of the hill to gain a vantage point. Keefe had told her he would be driving a station vehicle. He had been with the station vet for most of the morning but the vet had been scheduled to take a return helicopter flight at 1:00 p.m. to a neighbouring station. One hand shading her eyes, she stood and waited, twirling a bauhinia flower a shade restlessly between her fingers. A pair of kangaroos, a blue-grey female, considerably smaller, and a bright red male, a good six feet on its haunches, were indulging in a little love play down on the flats. The female was showing her affection by placing her short left arm across the male's broad back, tenderly kissing his muzzle. Sex, it seemed, made the world go round.

If only she had her camera! She was in her element here. The very nature of the landscape, with its great desert monuments, rock piles and stunning ramparts, its flora and extraordinary fauna, lent itself to spectacular shots. Kangaroos were fascinating to watch; large groups of them—as protection against dingo attack—getting around the countryside with their unique hops, standing up staring about while taking a break from grazing. Even the pugnacious males' battle for supremacy was thrilling, though it could become a life-and-death affair; two adult males fighting for the honour of taking off the desired female, leading the mob, mostly both.

Five minutes later she was rewarded by the sight of a Jeep speeding across the flat. The heavy tyres were sucking up the sand, sending up spiralling red willy-willies filled with grass seeds and grit.

The waiting was over! She felt such a tremendous rush of emotion she had difficulty swallowing… What she felt for Keefe was outside her control. Whatever happened—whatever the outcome of the DNA testing—she knew there would be no real future without him. But like many women before her faced with life-transforming trauma over an invisible oath given before God, she would have to stick with her religious beliefs. No one could ever say real life was easy.

He pulled her close, drawing her into his brilliant gaze. They kissed open-mouthed. Long sustained kisses. She kept nothing back. Neither did he.

This is what love is. The giving without stint.

It wasn't only her mouth and her arms she opened wide to him. She gave of her spirit. If she *had* to—if the worse came to the worst—she could live the rest of her life knowing she had once known a great love.

"There'll be protection in one of the caves," Keefe said urgently. He fixed his gaze on the hills with their innumerable caves and shelters. They desperately needed total privacy.

"The one with all the little stick people making love." She took his outstretched hand, her legs atremble. Aborigines over tens of thousands of years had been using rock facings for their art, drawing and incising carvings on countless rocky outcrops, some never seen by the white man.

The deep roomy cave Skye had chosen was full of hidden art. The drawings executed in a range of ochres. They could be understood immediately—men and women making love, beneath trees, alongside creeks with birds and cloud symbols overhead. The positions were very realistic. Even stick figures could bring a blush to the cheeks. Strikingly the male figures were wearing headdresses of birds' feathers.

This wasn't by any means the richest gallery on Djinjara, but it was one of the most accessible and it had a benign aura. It was no exaggeration for her to say the main gallery had the power to make the short hairs on her nape stand to attention. Tribal people believed a Dreamtime spirit had made its home there. She believed it too. She certainly wouldn't dare to photograph the rock drawings. Not that Keefe would allow her to. No one needed to bring the anger of the Great Ones down on their heads.

"How did it go with Scott?" She stood at the neck of the cave, watching Keefe check the thick yellow sand over. Little lizards scurried for cover, heading for the rock walls.

"Badly!" he threw over his shoulder.

A warning tremor shot through her. "Don't want to talk about it?"

"What is there to say?" He turned back to her, his silvery eyes contrasting strikingly with the deep bronze of his skin.

"Is he still blaming me?" She hadn't intended saying it but, despite that, it came out. There was just something in Keefe's expression that bothered her and spun resistance. She knew she had mulled far too long over that incident that had happened years ago.

"He's blaming you because he can't have you," Keefe said.

She shrugged as if it didn't matter, when it mattered a great deal. "Scott is the type who only wants what he can't have. He lets things fester in his mind."

"I know."

Waves of remembered resentment rose, making it difficult for her to speak. "So what are you going to do?" she asked. "Let worry over your brother affect our lives? He's not worth it, Keefe."

"I know that too," Keefe retorted grimly. "Falling in love with you was out of his control. I can surely understand. It was out of my control."

That jolted her heart. "Maybe I'm a witch!"

He gave a twisted half-smile. "You have powers. Don't let's talk about Scott any more," he said, his voice strained. "He's gone."

She let her fingernails dig into her palms. *Stop now. Keefe is right.* Instead, with the inbuilt perversity of women, she went at it. A fully fledged accusation. "So you can't have us both. Is that it, Keefe? Is that what's gnawing away at your heart? I can see you're upset. I understand it but I won't allow Scott to come between us. Some part of you thinks I have. That's the truth, isn't it?" She whipped out the challenge. "It will *always* be the truth. Scott won't change. We'll all die hoping."

His eyes burned over her and settled on her beautiful mouth. The most seductive woman's mouth he had ever seen. "Skye, please…let it go," he begged. "I can see all Scott's faults and failings but I love my brother. We're the same blood."

"What if *I* turn out to be the same blood?" She was passing beyond caution. "You're none too sure, are you? You and your grandmother."

That too she hadn't intended to say, but what the hell! She was in desperate need of reassurance. Torn between love and pride.

Keefe moved to her side, taking her firmly by the shoulders. "I've *told* you. I don't give a damn who you are. You're *my* Skye, my sun, moon and stars, my woman. You dazzle me. I love you more than anyone else on earth." He knotted a thick swathe of her hair around his hand, tipping back her head, hunger for her a different kind of torment. What was happening inside her he wasn't quite sure. All he knew was she was frantic about Jack and his well-being, just as he was worrying terribly about that crazy spontaneous vow she had made about giving him up as some sort of bargain with a God he didn't know if he believed in. The terrifying thing was, Skye *did.*

"I'm taking Dad back to Sydney," she told him quickly, the words crowding into her mouth. "You said he could have some time off.'

Keefe beat off frustration. He wanted her so badly he was in physical pain. "Of course he can. The break will do him good."

"We can get the paternity test done there." She was dismayed by the glacial tone of her voice. "Should take less than five working days. Then comes the denouement. He's my dad—the man who raised me, but not my biological father. I couldn't keep the results from him. He would want to see the results with his own eyes."

"Oh, for God's sake, let there be an end to it, Skye," Keefe raged. "This has to be settled once and for all. The *not* knowing is far worse than the knowing. I don't expect any revelations. Jack *is* your father. He *knows* how much you love him. I believe he'll hold up whatever the outcome."

"Then you're a darned sight more certain than I am. But, then, you're always so *sure*. Outcomes have to be what *you* want."

Her upraised hands were fluttering like agitated birds. He caught them. "I'm sure you love me, Skye. Nothing can obliterate that. But you're just superstitious enough to abandon me if you don't hear what *you* want. It's been a bad time for us both. I lost Dad. I'm trying to keep it all together. Then we lose Scott. It's *you* I can't lose. Is that clear? I can't bear to argue any more with you. There are supposed to be two theories for arguing with women anyway. I know from long experience of you that neither of them work. Life is full of obstacles. Together we can overcome them. No matter this business with Jack, what could be worse than for us to be parted?"

"Well, Jack's not *your* father, is he? Your answer seems to be that we just don't talk too much!" She was trying to tamp herself down, but fear and the heat of irrational anger was in her throat. Getting angry was a harsh relief. If only this whole business of paternity was a bad dream. She had no real faith her father could accept a negative outcome with any degree of serenity. An unwanted truth could kill him. Second time around. There was so much confusion in her mind, yet as they stood locked together, like a man and woman in combat, sizzling heat waves were rising all around them. The sparks could only billow into flame.

Keefe locked a steely arm around her, his eyes with a diamond-hard glint. "We don't talk," he muttered fiercely. "Talking is getting us nowhere. We make love."

She flung her long hair over her shoulder. "Go on, then! Shred my heart!"

So it was wordless, the well of desire bottomless.

Then came the gasps, the sharp little cries, the moans that went hand in hand with sexual excitement. He worked her out of her clothes, kissing every part of her creamy flesh as it became exposed. Tears streaked her cheeks. He licked them off. Each time her entered her, it was different. Nothing was quite like the last time. He was the most marvellous, accomplished lover, always astonishing her, showing her more and more things about herself, and her own body. Their love-making was becoming a long journey she hoped would never end. Two people could make their own magic; shut out the world.

The scent of him! The sweet, sweet flavour of his skin. Enormously complex feelings went into her surrender to the all-dominant male. He smelled tantalisingly of wood smoke and burnt eucalyptus leaves. She stared up into his brilliant eyes as his lean body covered hers, bearing down on her with a powerful, exultant rhythm. Her breasts, so satiated with feeling, were crushed beneath him. Her trembling legs were locked tight around him. She didn't know where she ended and he started. There was no distinction. They were two people, but one flesh. It was so piercingly perfect, nothing else mattered...

When it came time to leave Jack decided it was his duty to remain on Djinjara.

"Keefe needs me, sweetheart," he told Skye, an element of bravado in his voice. "Too much is laid on him. It's a killer job. I'm the overseer around here. I value my position. Besides, I'm as fit as a fiddle. You can see that. You go off with your samples and in due course you'll let me know."

Some note in his voice brought tears to her eyes. "Well, if that's what you want, Dad," she said gently. She could read his suffering.

"It is, love." Jack patted her shoulders with hands scarred by years of roping, fencing, mustering and other hard physical work. "I'm going to leave everything to you. I don't think I could bear the hanging around waiting, anyway. Far better for me to get back to work."

"If that's your decision, Dad. But you have nothing to agonise about. You're my dad, pure and simple. Don't fail me, Dad. I need you."

"Whatever the outcome, sweetheart, "Jack said, "I'll reconcile to it."

Except Skye knew he wouldn't.

Keefe had organised a private jet charter company to fly her back to Sydney, clipping hours off her time. Take-off was scheduled for 8:30 a.m. Another blazing blue day. Keefe drove her to the airstrip, which had been upgraded to accommodate small- to medium-size jets. The jet she was flying on could comfortably seat six passengers. There was to be one stop at Myall Downs to pick up a party of three cattlemen, all known to Skye, all Outback identities.

There was no exuberant display of love and affection between them. Rather an inflamed awareness and tension. Neither had the power to alter the outcome of this testing to suit their purpose. She felt perhaps unfairly that Keefe was scornful of the appeal she had made to the Almighty to save her father, and her subsequent vow. He might as well have been an atheist for the incredulous view he took of it. He wasn't bothering over much hiding it from her.

"Promises are often made under terrible stress. What sense is there in trying to hold to them?"

"I'd come with you if I could."

She shook her head. "You can't possibly get away. Look after Dad for me?"

"Jack is stronger than you think, Skye." He bent to kiss her, catching a burst of her special fragrance, wildflowers and sunshine. "Let me know the minute you have the results. *Before* Jack, naturally."

She gave a taut little smile. "We're all on tenterhooks about this, aren't we, no matter what we say?"

Keefe shook his head, crisply businesslike, if only on the outside. "No doubts or bothers from me. I love you. I need you. I refuse to let you go. I'm sure the Almighty has handled a lot of broken promises in His time. We have to put the past behind us, Skye."

Only the past would never die.

She delivered the samples for testing the same day. She had used this particular laboratory several times. It had an excellent reputation, fast, accurate and completely confidential.

"We'll have the results back to you by Friday, Ms McCory," the technician, Sarah, told her in her friendly fashion.

"I'd appreciate it."

She arrived back at the city building that housed her law offices, only to be confronted by a very angry-looking, burly middle-aged man, fast losing his hair.

God, here's trouble.

It never rained but it poured. His face looked familiar. Not a good face. An alcoholic's face. Ah, yes, Gordon Roth. A mean man. There were dangers that went along with representing women in distress. Like violent husbands who terrorised their wives and kids.

"Skye McCory?" He caught up with her, faded eyes

glaring. "You're the one that's been representing my wife, Emma. Emma Roth."

Skye stepped back a pace. "What is it you want, Mr Roth? You really shouldn't be talking to me."

"So high and mighty!" he sneered. "Think you've won over my wife, don't you? She wants a divorce. Good for you. Bad for me. You've made bad blood between us, lady. I can tell you that. Emma loves me. We can get back together."

Did such men ever learn? "I doubt very much if your wife is going to give you a fourth or is it a fifth chance, Mr Roth. And you can't tell me anything, so please step aside. Your wife has a restraining order in place against you for domestic violence. You had your chance to be heard at the court hearing. A *judge* decided to grant the restraining order to your wife. That could become permanent if you violate that order. You cannot harass or stalk me. You must understand that. Break the law and you could face imprisonment."

"The law! What's the law?" he shouted, waving his arms and drawing immediate attention to the two of them standing at the entrance to the building. "Stinking, rotten solicitors, the whole legal system is geared against men," he raged. "I'm no threat to Emma. Or the kids."

"Were that only true, Mr Roth. Allegations of abuse have been proven in court," she pointed out in a toneless voice. "Now, I really must go, but with a warning. Don't attempt to harass me. I promise you, you'll be sorry."

He gave her an evil look. "I know where you live."

One of the senior partners of the firm, coming out of the building, sized up the situation in an instant. "On your way, whoever you are!" she called in her most carrying, magisterial voice. "Skye, are you okay? Is this man harassing you?"

"He's on his way, Elizabeth. Aren't you, Mr Roth?"

He swore and made a crude gesture in their direction by way of goodbye.

"Sometimes we really do need protection," Elizabeth Dalkeith said very quietly and seriously, taking Skye's arm. Elizabeth had never fully recovered from seeing a family court judge shot dead right in front of her. "If that man gives you the slightest trouble—even a phone call—you're to let me know immediately."

"I will, Elizabeth. I promise."

Silently Skye prayed Gordon Roth would never show up again.

She had trouble concentrating on the outstanding files on her desk. Friday couldn't come soon enough. She knew it was normal enough to start harbouring doubts, especially when lives hung in the balance. Nevertheless, what she thought of as her disloyalty upset her intensely. She really was giving herself hell over all this. Keefe might believe—or chose to believe—his much-valued overseer could survive a tremendous emotional blow. She was far from sure. Another source of deep shame. She had started calling her dad *Jack* in her mind. Maybe with all this worry she was becoming very slightly unhinged?

Only there *had* been something between her mother and Jonty McGovern. Lady McGovern, a shrewd observer, couldn't have been that far out. What was more telling, Lady McGovern all these years hadn't let go of her belief that her son, Jonty, dead at twenty-two, had fathered Skye. Had no one else noticed an involvement? Keefe's father, Broderick? The rest of them, Keefe, Scott and Rachelle, had been children. She knew Keefe was deeply stressed when he allowed very little to stress him. He had a big job running the McGovern empire. He had also suffered the double loss of his father and brother.

Where had the idea of a conspiracy started? With Lady McGovern, of course. And yet Jack was convinced Cathy had loved him. Jack in his youth must have been a handsome man.

He was still a man women found attractive. There didn't have to be a conspiracy behind it. Through the days and the long restless nights she couldn't stop herself from going over and over different scenarios. Keefe wanted to marry her no matter what the outcome of the DNA testing was. There was no impediment after all, but her heart and soul were sore and shaking.

They had rescued Jack once. Would they be called on to do it again? Jack's whole life would implode with a negative outcome. So would hers, but such was her love for him that it was Jack she agonised about. Whatever the outcome, he, not Jonty McGovern, was her dad.

The results were delivered to her office in a large manila envelope marked *Confidential*. She heard voices in the corridor, a couple of her colleagues, so she rose swiftly and closed her door. She wanted no interruptions. She was far too much on edge to begin to hide it. Bracing herself, she opened the envelope. Her head was spinning dizzily. Too much coffee. Too little food.

She began to read. As she neared the bottom of the document, her nerveless fingers let go of the pages.

Skye bowed her blonde head and wept uncontrollably. Nobody could argue with a paternity test when it had a probability rating of ninety-nine point nine.

Keefe rode down to the yards where Jack and his aboriginal offsider, Chilla, were breaking in the best of the brumbies. Where Jack was tall and whipcord lean, Chilla was a small wiry man, both with a wonderful way around horses. They made a top team. The brumby they were breaking in when he arrived, a ghost grey, the sunlight dancing off his unkempt coat, was one of the mob that they had allowed to escape the day of the lightning strike. It was smallish in size, short legs, but powerful enough through the hind quarters. He waited until Jack had the quivering animal standing calmly on the sand, before gesturing to his overseer for his attention.

Jack ducked between the rails and came towards him, his lean, weathered face shadowed by the wide brim of his battered old Akubra, a flash of brilliant red from the bandana around his throat. "Yes, boss."

"I have some news for you, Jack."

"Oh, Gawd!" Jack's face started to work. But he stood in place, ramrod straight, a man receiving sentence. Normally so laid back, Jack was having the greatest difficulty gaining control of his emotions. Keefe put him out of his misery.

Jack swept off his dusty hat, throwing it so high in the air that several things happened at once. The brumby plunged, causing a lounging Chilla to spring to attention; scores of Technicolor parrots rose shrieking from the trees and a little mob of wallabies nearby bounded frantically to higher ground.

"Goddamn right!" Jack yelled. "I knew it. I knew it. My little Cathy would never have betrayed me."

Keefe put out his hand. Jack shook it. "You can't get anything clearer than that, Jack," Keefe said, enormously relieved to be the bearer of good news. "No argument from anywhere. Your belief in your wife—Skye's mother—has been totally vindicated. I'll have to talk to my grandmother. Set things straight. All these years she has laboured with entirely the wrong scenario firmly entrenched in her head. It's quite tragic." He gave a rueful smile.

"But now we *know*," Jack said, his expression so full of life and elation he looked ten years younger. "It was Jonty, you know, that was keen on Cathy. Not that I blamed him. She was like a ray of sunshine. He was so young. We were all so young. Poor Jonty!"

Keefe sighed. How little anyone knew what lay ahead in the future. "Let me say again how sorry I am my brother had to upset you."

Jack ducked his chin. "Upset us all. He sure did, boss,

but that's over. I really appreciate you coming to tell me. How's my girl?"

"My girl too, Jack." Keefe flashed a smile. "We talked for a long time on the phone." Indeed, their long conversation would always remain in his memory. The joy and the enormous relief in her voice, the outpouring of love. "I'm taking the weekend off to join her," he said, hugging the thought of their passionate reunion to him when in his own way he had been through hell. "Want to come along?"

Jack laughed aloud. He knew the score. "You don't need *me*," he said jovially. "I'll be seeing her soon. Give my beautiful girl—our beautiful girl—my love."

"Will do, Jack," Keefe said with a backward wave. He remounted his horse, riding away while Jack, on a wave of euphoria, turned back to his mate Chilla, calling, "Get the big one in here, Chilla, the roan. He's the pick of the bunch. Between the two of us we can turn him into a darned good working horse."

CHAPTER TEN

HE HAD to wait longer than he expected. It was dark now and the tenants who worked had had ample time to make their way home. Consequently, there was no movement around the entrance. He planned on slipping through the security door, either when someone entered or left the building.

Startling him—he was so engrossed in his plan—a taxi pulled up with a screech directly in front of the swish apartment complex. A young man on the hippy side got out, calling to someone still inside the taxi. "Check with Thommo. See you all around eight!"

While he watched and awaited his chance, the young man loped towards the entrance and Gordon Roth, waiting in the garden shadows, closed in quickly.

The security door opened at the click of a button. The young man became aware of the burly guy standing just behind him, almost breathing down his neck, definitely invading his space. Where in the heck had he come from? "You goin' in, mate?" He kept his tone relaxed. One didn't mess with a guy with a face like that.

"Yes," Gordon Roth leaned forward, crowding the young man further. "I was just about to buzz through to my friend.'

"What friend would that be, then, mate?" Something

about this burly guy was making the hitherto carefree young man uneasy.

"What's it to you?" Gordon Roth shot back, a flicker of rage in his eyes. "Anyway, she's waiting for me. We're going on to the theatre."

The young man's glance darted away. He hadn't missed that flicker. So much rage about these days. Road rage, home rage, work rage. A bad sign of the times. "So okay, then, enjoy yourself," he said, clearing his throat. The woman friend he reasoned must be pretty hard up. The guy looked as though he regularly gave women a belt in the mouth. He let the guy get away to the lift—he had no wish to go along for the ride—so he pulled out his mobile to feign a call. Anyway, the lady friend would have to be okay with the guy before letting him in.

Skye heard the knock on her door with a start. She wasn't expecting Keefe quite so early. But he was here! She had been busy preparing a meal for them both in the kitchen; a scallop salad for starters, and two lovely fresh Tasmanian salmon fillets served with marinated cucumber, avocado and green mango. Feeling extraordinarily elated, she moved with light, dancing steps to her front door.

Keefe! Every last impediment to their marriage had fallen away.

She didn't bother fixing her eye to the peephole. She threw open the door, a radiant welcoming smile in place.

"Oh, my God!" She stood transfixed, staring at her visitor with horror.

Find your breath. Steady up. Keefe is coming.

Gordon Roth loomed over her, one heavy foot in the doorway. "Shocked, are we?"

"Why wouldn't I be?" She knew a flash of outrage so intense she was able to summon a forceful tone: "Get away from my door, Mr Roth. I have a friend coming. He's with the police."

Fat fingers reached out to pinch her cheek. "I don't think

so, blondie. Let go of the door. I don't want to hurt you. Not for the next half-hour anyway. I'm here to talk. Let's keep this civilised."

"Civilised isn't breaking into my apartment," she answered sharply. "You could get into a lot of trouble over this."

"Trouble? I'm in enough trouble." Roth scowled, his blue eyes so faded they looked colourless. Pebbles. Dead.

"There's always more," Skye was quick to remind him. "You haven't been inside a jail as yet."

"Maybe I've been lucky!" He managed a laugh.

"And maybe your wife was too terrified of you to press charges. You won't bully me, Mr Roth. We've got nothing to say to each other. I strongly advise you to be on your way."

"You lawyers give a lot of advice." Abruptly he lashed out, pushing her backwards so she slammed into the hall console. "Let's go inside, shall we?" He got a painful grip on her arm, forcing her into the living room.

"Nice, nice!" His gaze swept the room. "How well you live! Now, everything will be fine, so relax. It was you who talked my wife into applying for a divorce. All you have to do now—if you know what's good for you—is convince her I'm worth another chance. I'm not letting my kids go. No way! They love me. Emma's a liar. She always was."

Skye was amazed at the calm disdain in her voice. "You can't talk to me about things like that, M. Roth. You must speak to your own solicitor. Kevin Barclay, isn't it?"

"Sacked 'im!" Roth said, thrusting his chin at her. "He was on my wife's side. Never said so, but even an idiot could tell."

"How did you get in here?" Skye took a pace away. *Keep him talking*. Keefe would soon arrive. Keefe could handle anything and anyone who came at him, even a snorting bull like Roth.

"People are careless." Roth waved the question away. "It was easy. Some young dude let me through."

"He shouldn't have done that. What did you say to him?"

"I said I was meeting up with a lady friend." Roth smirked.

"And you've had lady friends, haven't you, all through your marriage?" Skye stared back accusingly, one hand massaging her bruised spine.

Roth's expression turned grim. "You've been checking up on me, have you?"

Skye nodded. "Brothels, you name it."

"I don't do nothing other guys don't do. Especially guys who have a rabbit for a wife."

"Not even a rat could enjoy life with you," Skye said with contempt. She was getting a taste of what poor Emma had had to endure for years.

"A pity you said that!" The pebble eyes ran over her face and body. She was wearing a long halter-necked dress printed with flowers. He eyed her high, taut breasts, the skin that gave off light. "You're a real looker, aren't you? Never had a woman like you. I'm wondering what it would be like."

Her stomach flipped. What she saw in his eyes was *hate*. Not just for her. Or his hapless wife. For all women. She realised something terrible could happen to her. Gordon Roth was one step away from being crazy.

Behind them the phone in the kitchen rang, startling them both. "That will be my policeman friend."

"Leave it." Roth's warning was rough. "You heard me. Don't move."

She froze.

Another sound came on top of the strident ringing of the phone. A couple of raps on the front door.

Only one person it could be. *Keefe.* Immediately that steadied the wobbles that had invaded her limbs.

Seeing the change in her, Roth grabbed her, holding her body tightly in front of him like a hostage. As indeed she had become. They heard the door open.

"Not a good idea to leave the door unlocked, Sky-Eyes," Keefe called, his tone a mix of chiding and dead serious.

Skye drooped against Roth's restraining arm, overcome by relief. Then came fear, not just for herself but for Keefe. For all she knew, Roth might be carrying a gun.

"Care to step inside for a moment, Mr Policeman?" Roth's gravelly voice clanged metallically.

Keefe made a lightning response. He materialised in the living room like a genie materialised out of a puff of smoke. "Whoa!" He held up his hands, palms out, much as Skye had seen him steady a fractious horse. "What's going on here?"

"A little negotiation." Roth's face flushed a violent red.

"Okay," Keefe answered reasonably, acting on his judgment of the situation. "But first I suggest you let Ms McCory go." He held his furious anger well under control. "You're only making things worse for yourself, whoever you are. What are you doing here anyway?" As he spoke, Keefe advanced slowly but steadily, a tall, powerfully lean figure.

"I've got a weapon!" Roth yelled in an excited voice. "Like to see it?"

"Nice and slow," Keefe answered, sliding his hand inside his own jacket. "I have one too. Unluckily for you I'm a crack shot. I suggest, before this goes any further, you let Ms McCory go."

"Please, don't let any of us get hurt." Skye found her voice. "This is Gordon Roth, Keefe. I represent his wife. She has a restraining order in place against him for domestic violence. She wants a divorce."

"Now, why doesn't that surprise me?" Keefe said, moving to stand directly in front of them. "Let…her…go, Mr Roth." His tone was quiet, but every word carried tremendous weight.

To Skye's immense shock Roth caved in. He released her, using brute force to pitch her at Keefe, who fielded her deftly, taking a few seconds to steady them both.

Roth had his opportunity. He made for the door. Events were getting too much for him. He didn't have a weapon at all. The other guy did. Not that he would need it from the look of him. Oddly enough he didn't look like a copper, though he had an expression like granite.

Keefe had no difficulty closing in on him. He grabbed the back of Roth's shirt, bunching it and jerking him backwards. "Gotcha!"

Roth grunted in surprise. How had the cop moved so fast?

Keefe spun the big burly man like a steer, forcing him to the floor and planting a hard knee into his back. "Something to tie up his hands, Skye," he ordered, "or I could just knock him out. Funny about you bully boys," he mused, kneeing Roth harder. "You only target defenceless women."

Skye raced back with a length of picture cord she had on hand. "Sorry to be so long."

"No need to apologise. This will do nicely." Skilfully Keefe tied Roth's hands nice and tight. "You might give the police a call. This guy ought to be locked up."

"You can say that again!" Skye held a hand over her fast-beating heart.

Face down on the carpet, Roth was groaning in pain. "Are you gunna let me up?" Incredibly, he felt sorry for himself. He was in agony. The cop was using undue force, weighing down on him like a ton of cement bricks.

"No time soon," Keefe answered nonchalantly, when he badly wanted to smash Roth's face in. "Not hurting you, am I?"

Fiercely Roth got off a string of obscenities.

"Don't worry, when the police arrive, they'll let you up," Keefe consoled him. "That's the good part. The bad part is you'll be facing charges. Even then you can count yourself lucky, you truly worthless cur."

* * *

The police were at the door in under eight minutes. One of the officers handcuffed Roth, who, with a face screwed up as if he'd been mugged, protested violently about police brutality.

"He's not a copper, mate. Don't you know that?" the restraining officer said, keeping a straight face when he badly wanted to laugh.

Roth was led away and their statements taken. The police left with a warning: never open the door to anyone unless you know and trust them. They both seemed surprised they had to tell that to a lawyer. It was a lesson Skye would never forget. She knew more than anyone that there were a lot of angry, very frustrated people out there only too willing to take out their anger on anyone who got in their way.

"I was stupid," Skye admitted. She and Keefe were at last alone. "And once again you've had to come to my rescue."

They sat in silence for a moment, both their minds returning inevitably to the past and the distressing incident with Scott that had done all of them so much harm. Now the frightening encounter with Roth.

"Thank God I was there for you on both occasions," Keefe said on a fervent breath. "Deep as our bond has always been, we've moved ever closer over the years, if that's possible. No one will ever seek to harm you when I'm around."

"You were cast as my protector," she said, revelling in his role. "I thought it was you, of course, with Roth. I didn't even bother to check the peephole."

"That's what he was relying on." They sat together on the sofa, Keefe cradling her to him with one arm. Inside he was stunned by what had happened—what could have happened—to the woman he loved. On the outside he remained calm and supportive. "These guys that beat up their women have one thing in common. They're bullies for sure, but cowards most of all. Why do women continue to live with men who threaten them and their children? I don't get it."

His toying with her hair had gentled her exquisitely. Here was a man who could calm her at a touch, yet arouse her at will. "It would take a woman to be in that position to know. Murder-suicide is a fact of life. Women have to deal with that terrifying thought. Frustrated men turn psychotic. The frequency of it happening is shocking. Sometimes it seems to me I'm in a dangerous job. A few years back Judge Henry Rankin was shot dead outside the family law courts."

Keefe's frown deepened. Even with Roth in custody, the muscles at the back of his neck were still knotted with fury. "I remember you telling me that. One of your bosses was involved, wasn't she?"

Skye nodded. "Mercifully she was only a bystander, a friend of Judge Rankin's. She's never been the same since. Apparently the incident keeps coming back in flashes."

"I should think it would," he said grimly, his fears for her having sky rocketed. "Your boss must be one gutsy lady."

"She is." Abruptly her voice cracked and the held-back tears escaped onto her cheeks.

"Don't, *don't*, my love! I'm here. You're safe." Keefe pulled her across his lap. "I worry about you and what you do. Did you know that?"

"I worry about you too. It's pretty savage, what can happen on a cattle station." Day-to-day injuries, as she well knew. From time to time deaths.

"I can handle it. Which brings us to decision time. Are you completely happy to make a life change?" He waited intently for her answer. His need for her wasn't simply the overwhelming physical hunger he had for her. That was always present. But so many links went into making up their powerful bond. Now it was a question of dealing with their past experiences. They had resolved the most threatening issue, the one that had loomed so largely in tearing them apart, now it was time to discuss their hopes and goals for the future.

"Above anything I want you to be happy," Keefe said. "I want you to feel fulfilled not just as my wife and the mother of my children if we're so blessed, but as an individual in your own right. You hold down a difficult, demanding job in keeping with your high intelligence. Is it conceivable, do you think, my love, you could become bored and restless with too much time on your hands?"

"Bored?" She turned up her head. "On Djinjara?"

"Well, I know you love it." He dropped a glowing kiss on her mouth. "But—"

"No buts," she said, easing back voluptuously into his strong male body. "Have you forgotten my interest in photography?" she teased.

"Not at all. But how serious is it? I know you have exceptional talent."

"Why thank you, kind sir!"

"Okay. You know I'll help you in every way I can. Your happiness is paramount. Everyone marries with the hope of being happy. Not every marriage survives."

She sat straight. "Listen, what are you trying to do, put me off?"

"God, no!" He actually shuddered. "What a thought!"

"You're thinking about your mother and father?"

"How could I not!" he replied, rather bleakly. "My parents' marriage wasn't a great success. You know that."

"But the great thing we have in our favour, Keefe, is that I'm Djinjara born and bred. I love our desert home as much as you do. It's taken overlong, but we've finally sorted out the ghosts of the past. You've told me your grandmother and Rachelle want our marriage to go ahead?" She searched his brilliant eyes.

"I don't intend to be wafted off by flights of angels until I see my first grandchild." Keefe reported his grandmother's

words verbatim. "Rachelle almost broke my heart asking very tentatively did I think you might allow her to be a bridesmaid."

"Wh-a-t?" Skye was betrayed into saying sharply, then quickly recovered. "And what did you answer?" She modified her tone. Keefe's family would be her family.

"I'm sure she'll want you, I said. Did I do wrong?" He gave her a down-bent mocking smile.

"No, of course you didn't. But that's only because I love *you* so fiercely." Skye returned to burrowing her head into the curve of his shoulder. "I'll love you until my dying breath."

"Hey, no talk about dying," Keefe protested. He was still feeling shock waves over Roth. With an urgent hand he swept her hair to one side so he could press kisses down the column of her neck. "You can never stop living. With *me*."

"So why don't we get married right away?" She was only half joking. She didn't think she could bear to be parted from him for another second.

"Okay with me!" he answered without hesitation, then paused, his expression thoughtful. "But not, I think, with all the people who will want to come to our wedding. Anyway, *think,* my one and only love. You can't possibly deprive me of the sight of my beautiful bride in all her regalia. I will want all the trimmings."

The depth of feeling in his voice would have made any prospective bride deliriously happy. She was over the moon. The future she had been so desperate about was now set. "And you'll get all the trimmings," she vowed, her mind woman-like already running ahead. "The glorious wedding gown— it will cost a fortune—the long veil, the train, the hand-made wedding shoes, something borrowed, something blue, the most exquisite bridal bouquet. Four bridesmaids. Two flower girls." It was all coming to life as she spoke. Designs, colours. "A magnificent Djinjara setting. Reception in the Great Hall."

"God, I can't wait!" Keefe pulled her ever nearer.

"Neither can I!" Her answer was a peal of joy. "Dad is at peace with the news?"

Keefe pressed a kiss to the blue pulse in her temple. "Just like I said. I invited him to come along but he said the two of us wouldn't need him. He sends his love for now. Finally his Cathy, your mother, has found her rightful place in our lives."

"Lord be praised!" For a moment Skye experienced in amongst the joy a sharp sense of loss. She would have given anything to have a few beautiful memories of her mother. Even a *single* memory. Very sadly that had not been her lot.

"It hasn't been easy for you, has it?" Keefe asked gently, as ever reading her mind.

"I always had *you*." There was a deeply emotional catch in her voice. "The great bond we shared has helped me through life."

"I feel exactly the same." That was Keefe's simple answer.

"Our children will be born out of love," she said.

"Indeed they will!" He joined his mouth to hers. It was more than an intense kiss. It carried a solemn vow.

"And Lady Margaret is happy we're *not* first cousins?" she breathed against his lips, unable to resist the sliver of irony.

"Cousins? God, girl, you're my *twin*, my other half," he cried. "Believe me, Gran is thrilled. A great burden has been lifted off her frail shoulders. She meant it when she said she was going to stick around until she can hold our first child in her arms."

"And the one after that," Skye said, her happiness absolute. Her vision had such clarity. The two of them making their journey hand in hand through life. Partners. Full partners. In every way. It filled her mind with glory. "I suppose it would be too much to hope Scott can get his act together?" She briefly sobered.

"You said it, Sky-Eyes." Keefe's answer was laconic. "Scott's a man in charge of his own future. I guess he has a perfect right to go to the devil if he so chooses. We'll just have to make do with the entire McGovern clan plus most of the Outback."

"Wonderful!" She was floating high again on emotion. "Only you haven't officially asked me to marry you.".

"Watch this!" Before she knew what he was about, he tumbled her off his lap, falling to one knee on the plush rug, taking her hand. He turned it over, spread her palm wide. Then he bent his raven head to press an ever-deepening kiss into her palm. It sent little electric jolts all over her highly receptive body. "How old were you when you first asked me to marry you?" There was devilment in his eyes. "Five, wasn't it?"

She gave a little laugh, her expression both tender and alluring. "I was always a precocious child and you were always my prince. You used to call me 'little buddy'."

"You *were* my little buddy then. Now you're my woman, soon to be my wife. I can love you and take care of you better than any other man on earth."

"You'd better!" she teased, exhilaration in her eyes.

"Oh, I will." He leaned forward to kiss her lips, luscious as strawberries, taking his own good time. Slowly…very slowly… drawing the tip of his tongue over the pillowy contours, tracing the outline…all the while feeding her hunger….

Her arms draped themselves around his neck. "You're the best kisser in the world," she exulted. "The *best*!"

"And we're not finished yet," he said with thrilling ardency. "Skye Catrina McCory, will you do me the great honour of becoming my bride?" He stared into her eyes, thinking them the most beautiful blue he had ever seen. His daughters simply *had* to have eyes like that. "Would you please raise your left hand?"

"Right hand for the Bible." She tried to laugh, but there was a decided shake to it.

"Left hand for engagement rings," he pointed out.

She threw her head back in surprise. "You haven't *got* one surely?"

"Not on my person, no. But give me a moment." He sprang up with characteristic litheness, moving across to where his jacket was folded over an armchair.

"Quickly, quickly!" She gave in to a helpless moan. "The suspense is killing me."

He came back to her, and then with an exaggerated courtly flourish knelt at her feet. "I had hoped things would go more perfectly tonight—"

"Don't you dare speak about Gordon Roth," she cried, love and longing rising high in her breast. "I'm not going to allow a miserable creature like him mar our great moment."

"I should think not! *Voilà!*" He opened up a small box covered in dark blue velvet. "Name me one beautiful blue-eyed woman who doesn't have—or should have—a magnificent sapphire?" he challenged. "You think it's beautiful?" His gaze, earnest and intense, sought her approval.

"Oh, Keefe!" She made a little sound of awe and heady delight. "It's *so* beautiful. I'm going to need all night to tell you."

"Don't worry, I'll keep you awake so you can," he promised, silver eyes glinting. Gently he slid the exquisite sapphire and diamond ring down over her knuckle into its resting place. "With this ring I seal our pact. Together we walk through life hand in hand. Man and wife."

"A big amen to that!" She answered on a prayerful breath. The high sense of occasion was accompanied by overwhelming emotion, blocking her throat with tears. "It's very scary, loving you so much," she confessed.

He answered with raw emotion. "My darling, you scare me, too. That's what comes of loving so intensely." He reached for her hungrily, drawing her down onto the rug beside him. Gently he settled her on her back, loving the way her honey-blonde hair fanned out around her flushed, excited face, pulsing with light. "I want to look at you. I want to love you." For long moments he placed his hands on either side of her head, staring down at her.

"Now can't be soon enough!" The heat of passion was making its blistering path from her head to her toes.

"So what do you think?" His voice was as smooth and rich as molten honey. "Will I make love to you here, or will I carry you down the hallway to bed?"

For answer Skye threw up her slender arms, ecstatically locking them around his neck and drawing his beloved head down to her. She was literally thrumming with love and desire.

"Here is *perfect* for me," she said.

* * * * *

Harlequin offers a romance for every mood!
See below for a sneak peek
from our paranormal romance line,
Silhouette® Nocturne™.
Enjoy a preview of REUNION
by USA TODAY bestselling author Lindsay McKenna.

Aella closed her eyes and sensed a distinct shift, like movement from the world around her to the unseen world.

She opened her eyes. And had a slight shock at the man standing ten feet away. He wasn't just any man. Her heart leaped and pounded. He reminded her of a fierce warrior from an ancient civilization. Incan? She wasn't sure but she felt his deep power and masculinity.

I'm Aella. Are you the guardian of this sacred site? she asked, hoping her telepathy was strong.

Fox's entire body soared with joy. Fox struggled to put his personal pleasure aside.

Greetings, Aella. I'm the assistant guardian to this sacred area. You may call me Fox. How can I be of service to you, Aella? he asked.

I'm searching for a green sphere. A legend says that the Emperor Pachacuti had seven emerald spheres created for the Emerald Key necklace. He had seven of his priestesses and priests travel the world to hide these spheres from evil forces. It is said that when all seven spheres are found, restrung and worn, that Light will return to the Earth. The fourth sphere is here, at your sacred site. Are you aware of it? Aella held her breath. She loved looking at him, especially his sensual mouth. The desire to kiss him came out of nowhere.

Fox was stunned by the request. *I know of the Emerald Key necklace because I served the emperor at the time it was created. However, I did not realize that one of the spheres is here.*

Aella felt sad. Why? Every time she looked at Fox, her heart felt as if it would tear out of her chest. *May I stay in touch with you as I work with this site?* she asked.

Of course. Fox wanted nothing more than to be here with her. To absorb her ephemeral beauty and hear her speak once more.

Aella's spirit lifted. What *was* this strange connection between them? Her curiosity was strong, but she had more pressing matters. In the next few days, Aella knew her life would change forever. How, she had no idea....

Look for REUNION
by USA TODAY *bestselling author Lindsay McKenna,*
available April 2010, only from Silhouette® Nocturne™.

HARLEQUIN® Romance®

ROMANCE, RIVALRY
AND A FAMILY REUNITED

THE BRIDES
of
BELLA ROSA

William Valentine and his beloved wife, Lucia, live
a beautiful life together, but when his former love Rosa
and the secret family they had together resurface,
an instant rivalry is formed. Can these families
get through the past and come together as one?

———————

*Step into the world of Bella Rosa
beginning this April with*

Beauty and the Reclusive Prince
by
RAYE MORGAN

Eight volumes to collect and treasure!

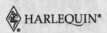

LARGER-PRINT BOOKS!

GET 2 FREE LARGER-PRINT NOVELS PLUS
2 FREE GIFTS!

From the Heart, For the Heart

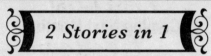

2 Stories in 1

HER MEDITERRANEAN PLAYBOY

Sexy and dangerous—he wants you in his bed!

The sky is blue, the azure sea is crashing
against the golden sand and the sun is hot.

The conditions are perfect for
a scorching Mediterranean seduction
from two irresistible untamed playboys!

Indulge your senses with these two delicious stories

A MISTRESS AT THE ITALIAN'S COMMAND
by *Melanie Milburne*

ITALIAN BOSS, HOUSEKEEPER MISTRESS
by *Kate Hewitt*

Available April 2010 from Harlequin Presents!

Coming Next Month

Available April 13, 2010

#4159 TOUGH TO TAME
Long, Tall Texans
Diana Palmer

#4160 BEAUTY AND THE RECLUSIVE PRINCE
The Brides of Bella Rosa
Raye Morgan

#4161 MARRYING THE SCARRED SHEIKH
Jewels of the Desert
Barbara McMahon

#4162 ONE SMALL MIRACLE
Outback Baby Tales
Melissa James

#4163 AUSTRALIAN BOSS: DIAMOND RING
Jennie Adams

#4164 HOUSEKEEPER'S HAPPY-EVER-AFTER
In Her Shoes...
Fiona Harper

HRCNMBPA0310